MW00618702

Holidays in Manhattan

Holidays in Manhattan

A McKinnon Brothers Romance

Jennifer Gracen

TULE
PUBLISHING

Holidays in Manhattan
Copyright© 2019 Jennifer Gracen
Tule Publishing First Printing, October 2019

The Tule Publishing, Inc.

ALL RIGHTS RESERVED

First Publication by Tule Publishing 2019

Cover design by Lee Hyat at www.LeeHyat.com

No part of this book may be used or reproduced in any manner whatsoever without written permission except in the case of brief quotations embodied in critical articles and reviews.

This is a work of fiction. Names, characters, places, and incidents are products of the author's imagination or are used fictitiously. Any resemblance to actual events, locales, organizations, or persons, living or dead, is entirely coincidental.

ISBN: 978-1-951190-50-7

Dedication

For my close friend, Jeannie Moon. You know all the reasons why. But at the very least, this book probably wouldn't have happened without your input and support.

And for all those who believe in or hope for some magic at the holidays, no matter what you celebrate.

Acknowledgments

First and foremost, thank you so much to Meghan Farrell and Jane Porter, and the whole Tule team, for your continuous support and enthusiasm for this whole series. You're the best.

Thank you, Sinclair Sawhney, for being a lovely editor yet again. Four out of five! (books, not stars)

Thank you, Stephany Evans, my fantastic agent, who believes in me and my work.

Thank you, Lee Hyat, for yet another gorgeous cover! You're a magician.

Thank you to Nika Rhone, Patty Blount, and Nicole Tynan for beta reading. Thank you to Jeannie Moon and Lauren Rico, for pushing, brainstorming, and simultaneous hugs and smacks upside my head. And thanks to all five of you for being wonderful friends.

Thank you, The Quillies, for never ending laughs and support.

Thank you, Mom, always, for everything.

Thank you, Justin, for giving me desperately needed reminders and some inspiration while I was writing this story. DAMN RIGHT.

Most of all, thank you, dear readers, for taking some time to escape into my book. I hope you enjoy this finish to the McKinnon Brothers series! I truly appreciate you so much.

Chapter One

ANNA WAS GOING to be late. But really, it wasn't totally her fault; she was notoriously not a morning person and everyone knew that, she'd woken up late to begin with, and she couldn't walk by the bakery window when those gorgeous cupcakes were practically shouting at her. The miniature red, orange, and yellow sugary leaves on top were so inviting, she couldn't squelch the urge to get two of them for her nieces. It was a very good excuse for being a few minutes late to brunch. Especially when she so rarely did a Sunday brunch.

After working until two A.M. the night before, as she often did, Sundays were for being lazy, running a few errands, and laundry. Since she worked evening and night shifts at her brother's bar, she rarely saw the sun before noon in general. But she'd been summoned by her sister-in-law, who'd become a cherished friend besides a member of the McKinnon family, and Anna hated to deny Cassandra anything.

Three days ago, Anna had turned thirty-one. Cass had insisted on a family get-together to celebrate her birthday.

Most of the tremendous McKinnon family was back in Ireland, where Anna and Sean had been born and raised. Here in New York City, Sean, Cassandra, and their daughters were the only family Anna had around. She cherished them all, but was unabashedly in love with her nieces. Sweet Rose was five, and Ella, only twenty-one months old, was already a firecracker.

Since Anna worked nights, dinner for her birthday hadn't been an option. So, now, a birthday brunch for Anna was happening... whether she liked it or not.

Yawning as she adjusted her wide sunglasses, Anna squinted against the glare of the sun before turning to glance through the bakery window. Almost empty at noon on a Sunday, there was only one other person in line, so she wouldn't have to wait long—and therefore wouldn't be too late to brunch. Always one to fly with her impulses, she entered the bakery.

A bell tinkled over the door as Anna pushed through it, and immediately the sweet smell of sugar bombarded her senses. She'd never been in this small bakery before, though she'd passed it many times. She passed this place every time she walked across town to get to Sean and Cassandra's apartment. They'd moved to a small but charming place in the West Village three years before, and Anna adored their neighborhood. It had character, it had style... not unlike where Anna lived in the East Village, but it was just a different vibe. More families lived in the West Village, so it was a good place to raise the girls. It was also closer than they'd been to NYU, where Cassandra worked as an English Lit professor. Anna visited them often. It was all too easy to feel isolated in the huge city; along with a few friends, having some family there kept her from feeling adrift.

As Anna waited, she smiled as she thought of her nieces. Those two little girls would squeal with delight when they saw the pretty cupcakes. She'd do anything for them. They owned her heart. She hoped to have kids of her own one day, but since her dating life was a joke, she was more than happy to glom onto her brother's kids. Anna had always been a free spirit, as well as a bartender who worked nights, and had high standards—all of which made real dating difficult. Hookups were easy if that were all she wanted, but it wasn't. She'd seen true love up close and wanted it for herself one day. But even being in one of the biggest cities on the planet, it was hard to meet people.

Sean and Cassandra had the real thing. After years together, the heated way they still looked at each other sometimes was enough to set off fire alarms. A few years ago, her other brother, Gavin, had come to visit her in New York and fallen head over heels for Toni, one of her friends. They were so in love that Toni had left her life on Long Island to start a new one with Gavin over in Dublin.

Though she'd never admitted it to anyone out loud, Anna wanted that. That knock-you-on-your-ass kind of love, the passion and the devotion, the feeling of finding your kindred spirit. Her schedule was crazy, sure, but being a bartender in midtown Manhattan had its perks. She met plenty of men. Just none that knocked her off her axis.

She'd been in love before, but... she rolled her eyes at herself just thinking about those failed relationships. Maybe she'd be an auntie for life.

"Can I help you?" The voice of the woman behind the counter broke into her thoughts, jarring her back to the present as the customer in front of Anna turned to leave with her box of goodies.

"Yes, thanks," Anna said, taking off her sunglasses. "Those gorgeous cupcakes in the window—" She reached up and back to point to them and connected hard with flesh.

"Ooof!" came a deep voice from behind her.

Gasping, Anna whirled around in horror. The man standing behind her held his face as he glared down at her. "Oh sweet Jesus," she stammered. "I punched you in the face, didn't I?"

"Mm hmm," he ground out.

"I'm so sorry. I didn't even know you were there!"

"Yeah, I got that."

She quickly took in his dignified appearance: navy suit, crisp white shirt, striped tie, his head full of wavy dark hair, and the way his eyes narrowed as they raked over her. Incredible eyes, the color of expensive whiskey, but sharp and clearly annoyed. She tried to joke, "I'm not usually in the habit of clocking people."

"I'd hope not." His words were muffled behind his hand, but his clipped tone was unmistakable.

No sense of humor, she thought. *Pity.* "I really am sorry. Are you all right?"

"I'll live," he muttered, slowly pulling his hand away from his face. A drop of blood welled on his full bottom lip.

"Ah Christ, look what I did." Anna turned back to the woman behind the counter, who was watching them with wide eyes. "D'ya have a napkin, love? He needs one."

"Of course!" The woman grabbed a few and handed them to Anna, who turned to try to dab at his mouth.

He grabbed her wrist with surprising speed. "I can do that."

A lance of embarrassment pierced through her and she shook off his hand. "I was just trying to help," she said.

He blinked, then sighed. "I know. Sorry." He took a napkin from her fingers and held it to his lip. "I'm fine. Go on, place your order. I have a meeting I have to get to."

"On a Sunday?" Anna couldn't help but ask.

"Yes." He stared at her, but didn't offer more.

She held his intense gaze for a long beat. His eyes were truly stunning, a golden hazel fringed with black lashes, in the middle of an appealing face. A strong jaw, cleanly shaven. His thick hair was such a dark brown it was almost black, the waves cut short and neat. A lawyer, she figured, or some kind of finance guy. Whatever. Not her type, and not her concern. He said he was fine, and he wasn't being friendly. She turned back to the woman behind the counter and asked for two of the cupcakes she'd seen in the window.

While she waited, she pushed her hair over her shoulder, leaned a hip against the counter, and shot a glance back at the man she'd assailed. She couldn't help herself. Damn, he was cute. "You okay?"

"Fine." He pulled the napkin away and his tongue flicked out to touch his lip. Something in her belly pinged low. He had a gorgeous mouth, with full sensual lips. Delicious lips, really.

She caught how his whiskey-colored eyes quickly ran over her, but his expression didn't change a bit. Not a flicker of anything. She supposed he wasn't impressed by what he saw. Suits didn't go for women like her. She knew that all too well.

She turned her back on him to stare at the wall of assorted cookies.

As soon as her purchase was paid for, she grabbed the box and brushed by him, not bothering to say anything else. He obviously felt nothing but scorn toward her, and she'd apologized more than once, so what was the point? She pushed through the door and walked out into the brisk air.

She'd only gotten about twenty feet up the block when she heard someone shouting behind her, "Hey! Blondie with the colors! Wait!"

Realizing someone was yelling at *her*—her blonde hair had streaks of orange and black through it, the colors she'd picked for October—she turned around to see the guy she'd hit in the bakery, jogging to her. When he reached her, he held out an ATM card and said, "You left this there."

Anna glanced down and plucked it from his long fingers. Sure enough, it was hers. "Christ," she hissed, embarrassed in front of this man for the second time in only a few minutes. Her cheeks burned a bit as she admitted, "I was in such a hurry to get away from you, I didn't even realize…"

"I figured as much," he said. He swiped a hand through his hair, tousling the waves. "I'm sorry for being such a dick back there. You punched me, and it hurt, and I was in a pissy mood to begin with because I don't want to have to go to a meeting on a Sunday." The corner of his full mouth ticked up the slightest bit. She figured that was this stiff's attempt at a smile.

He was wound up tight, buttoned up and reserved. The guy probably needed a strong drink. Or a good time. She wondered when was the last time he'd had either one. "Well. I appreciate your chasing me down to give me this." She waved her bank card at him, then reached into her messenger bag for her wallet and tucked it inside. "And I appreciate your apology too. I really didn't mean to—"

When she looked back up at him, what she spotted just beyond him made her eyes go wide and her breath stick in her chest. "Damn," she whispered. Ethan, her ex who'd broken her heart a year and a half ago, was walking up the street. The lying bastard was only yards away. Too late to make a smooth escape. Panic made her heart flutter before it started to race. She licked her suddenly dry lips.

"You okay?" the suit asked, his thick brows furrowing as he looked at her.

"Um. No. Yes. Shit." Struck with an idea, she grabbed his wrist. "Can you do me a *huge* favor?" she whispered hotly.

Looking down at her like she was insane, he said with ambivalence, "Uh… depends what it is?"

"My name is Anna," she said, shifting the box of cupcakes to her left hand. "Just work with me." Her right arm hooked around his neck, she pressed herself against his body, and brought his mouth down to crash onto hers.

Chapter Two

D AVID'S HEAD WAS spinning. One moment, this wild girl, a total stranger, was talking to him and looking annoyed—the next, she'd grabbed him and was kissing him. Not knowing what the hell was happening, his whole body went rigid. Then he was flooded with something he hadn't recognized in too long a time: desire. An undeniable spark and flare. This beautiful woman was kissing him on the street, in front of the whole world, and she felt damn good pressed up against him.

"Just work with me," she'd whispered desperately.

Okay. The hell with it. He wrapped an arm around her waist and kissed her back.

Falling into the kiss was easy. Hell, he'd noticed her as soon as he'd stepped into the bakery and taken his place in line behind her. It was hard not to. The woman was a burst of color. Streaks of black and orange in her shoulder-length blonde hair, a walking billboard for Halloween in two days. She wore red and blue patterned leggings, and the pale slope of her shoulder peeked from her cutout-shoulders bright blue top. The tattoo on her right shoulder was of hot pink flowers and an emerald vine that crept back down into her shirt. He was gazing down at her skin, wondering how far down the vine went and where it ended, when she cracked him right in the face.

He'd been stunned by the blow, caught so off guard that when she whirled around in obvious horror, he'd all but growled at her. Then his heart skipped a beat. She was gorgeous. High cheekbones, perfect skin, tiny diamond stud in her nose, and the bluest eyes he'd ever seen in his life. They were a dark but brilliant blue, and so striking they stopped him cold. His breath got stuck in his lungs.

She said something and he picked up on her accent—Irish, maybe? There was a slightly lyrical lilt to her speech he found enchanting. Then embarrassment seared him as he realized the truth was, if he hadn't been ogling her from behind so blatantly, her hand might've only skimmed his chin instead of clocking him right in the mouth. An added bonus was he now might be late for his conference call, which he'd resented having to take on a Sunday in the first place. He'd snapped at her as a result, and she'd been clearly irritated by his inability to accept her apology graciously. Not his best moment.

It was no wonder she'd left in a huff... but the cashier had called out to her as the door closed behind her. Realizing the situation, he'd grabbed the bank card without thinking, promising the cashier he'd get it to her as he raced out of the bakery.

Now this feisty, colorful, tattooed woman was kissing him. Pressing her soft, enticing body against him, slender arm hooked around his neck, warm mouth sealed to his. A spark went off between them, flaring into heat. Shifting slightly, he angled his mouth to deepen the kiss and her mouth opened for him. His tongue touched hers, warm and greedy, and he felt her gasp into his mouth. A surge of lust shot through him. The kiss got hotter.

But just as he started to enjoy the moment, a man's voice next to him said in surprise, "Anna? Is that you?"

She pulled away from David, blinking as she said, "Ethan. My God. Fancy running into you, of all people." She stayed close to David's side, sliding her arm around his waist and looking up at him. "Sweetheart, this is Ethan. The rotten ex I told you about."

David always came to a rescue if needed. Playing along without hesitation, he held her tightly to his side, running his hand up and down her arm as he gave Ethan his most withering glare. "That's unfortunate. But hey, his loss is my gain, isn't it?"

Anna smiled, and it was as bright as the sun above. "Sweet talker. Yeah, you got that right."

Ethan scowled. "Anna… you know, I—I never got to fully explain. You didn't let me. You wouldn't answer my calls or my texts."

"Why would I?" she asked, a bite in her tone.

"Because…" Ethan squirmed a bit. "I never meant to

hurt you."

"Right," she said. "You also never meant to tell me about your *wife*. Found that one out the hard way, didn't I? Running into you with your wife and kids was such a joy. Not to mention how you acted like you didn't even know me."

David's eyes flew to her face. Ah hell. No wonder she needed an assist. "Babe," he said to her in an affectionate tone, "don't give him another thought. We have a great life together. Past is the past."

Her gaze locked on his and her smile returned. God, she was even more beautiful when she smiled. "You're wonderful," she murmured. Then she shot Ethan a look that could have frozen lava and said curtly, "Bye."

Ethan stared at her for a few seconds, then shook his head and stalked off.

David felt her body relax against him and asked, "You okay?"

"Stellar," she said, pulling away. She grinned up at him. "You were perfect. Really. Thank you so much for that."

He shrugged. "No problem. It was... kind of fun."

Her thin brows shot up. "If that was fun, you need to get out more."

Snorting out a laugh, he admitted, "You're not wrong. I work like seventy hours a week. Sometimes more."

"Well... I owe ya." She reached into her bag and searched with one hand, then pulled out a pen and the receipt from the bakery. Leaning it against the box of cupcakes, she scribbled on it as she said, "You were a right hero just now. I owe you for that. So here... this is the bar I work at. You ever come in, I'll buy all your drinks for a night. And who knows, you might have some fun, too."

She held out the receipt and he took it. Glancing at it, she'd written *O'Reilly's Tavern, 46th & Fifth* and her name beneath it. He looked back up at her. "You know, I might take you up on that sometime."

"You should. I mean it. It's the least I can do." She tossed the pen back into her bag. A breeze lifted her hair, making the ends dance, and she pushed it out of her eyes. "I work Tuesdays through Saturdays, from five to midnight. Often later on Saturdays."

"Okay."

"Okay. Maybe I'll see ya, then."

"Question," he said.

"Answer?" She cocked her head, grinning wickedly.

He couldn't help but grin back. "Your accent. Faint, but definitely there. Where are you from?"

"Ireland," she said. "Followed one of my older brothers here seven years ago, been here ever since. Hence the 'faint'."

"Ah. I wondered."

She gazed at his mouth. "Hope I didn't hurt your lip too badly, between the punch and the kiss."

He chuckled and shoved his hands in his pockets. "I'm fine."

"Oh good." She pulled sunglasses out of her bag and put them on. "Well, you have a meeting to get to, and I'm late for brunch."

"Try not to slug anyone on your way there," he joked.

She stilled, a sweet smile blooming on her face. "And here I thought you didn't have a sense of humor."

His brows shot up. "Ouch."

Now she was the one who laughed. "Hey, what's your name, anyway?"

"David." He held out his hand. "David Beren."

"You're a good white knight, David," she said as she shook his hand. "A good kisser too." Shooting him a wink and a saucy grin, she turned and began walking. "That drink offer stands!" she called over her tattooed shoulder. "No expiration date!"

He watched her walk away, watched how the sun brought out the many hues of her hair, making them glow, and the hypnotic sway of her narrow hips. She was a blur of color and energy… and he couldn't stop grinning. He pulled out his wallet, tucked the receipt into it, and turned to head back to the bakery. No way was he getting through a boring conference call without one or two of Sweet Lovin' Bakery's cinnamon rolls.

IT HAD BEEN a long damn week. David stared out the window of his office, twenty-eight floors above midtown

Manhattan. This was the first time he'd finished before ten P.M. in two weeks. He took off his reading glasses, rubbed his tired eyes, and leaned back in his leather chair. He knew he should go home and try to get some sleep, but he was still too wired. The adrenaline rushes he got while working were what got him through the long days.

This was the life he'd pursued. His father had been an investment banker, enabling Howard Beren to provide a good life for his family. David's older brother, Jacob, went to med school, leaving David to pick up the mantle of keeping finance in the family. Luckily for David, he was great with numbers and actually wanted to follow in his father's esteemed footsteps.

David had been laser-focused since junior high. He was salutatorian in high school, went to Cornell for undergrad, and Wharton for his MBA. He'd snared a job with The Linderton Group before he'd even graduated, and his career had taken off from there. The work-hard, play-hard life of an investment banker suited him. He wanted it, he went after it with dogged determination, and he was successful.

But now, at thirty-five, sometimes he wished the long days and weeks weren't quite so long. The payoff was great, but he would've liked to enjoy his personal life a little more. Hell, if he had more of a personal life. His career dominated his time. He'd always dated sporadically, but his schedule hadn't really left time for a relationship. Or maybe, he just hadn't met someone special enough that he wanted to commit to. The one serious relationship he'd had that went the distance had crumbled under the weight of his long hours. And, when push came to shove—or rather, when Kimberly pushed for a ring and David realized he didn't want to marry her—that had been that.

His parents had been married for forty-one years. They still adored each other. They were fiercely loyal to and brought out the best in one another. Unless David found someone like that, he intended to stay single.

Maybe one day. Maybe not. Right now, he'd be happy to have someone he was even remotely interested in. He and Kimberly had ended three years ago, and there'd been no one special since. Empty sex was available, but lately it left him feeling just that: empty. Maybe he was ready for something... more.

His cell phone rang and he automatically picked it up without even looking at the caller ID. "Beren."

"Why are you still at work?" his mother asked. "It's so late."

"Hi, Mom." David leaned back even further in his seat, relaxing a bit. "I always work late."

"But not *this* late," Susan said. "It's nine-thirty, honey. Have you had dinner?"

He couldn't help but smile. "Still checking on me."

"I'm your mother, that's my job. And you didn't answer me."

"I ordered in a sandwich a few hours ago. I ate," he assured her. He scrubbed a hand over his face and felt the scratch of heavy end-of-day stubble along his jaw.

"Okay, good."

"So what's up?"

"Just checking about plans," Susan said. "Thanksgiving is just a few weeks away. Are you coming in on Wednesday night and staying over, or are you just coming in on Thursday morning? And are you staying through the weekend?"

"Um…" David reached for his water bottle with his free hand. "I'll come out on Thursday morning." He stole a quick sip. "And I'm staying over on Friday for sure, but don't know about the whole weekend. Depends on work. We'll see. Is that okay?"

"Absolutely."

"When are Jacob, Sharon, and the kids coming?"

"Thursday morning."

"Okay." David hadn't seen his older brother since the High Holidays. "So don't worry, you'll have a full house."

"I can't wait. Haven't since September. That's too long."

"Well, you will before you know it." He capped the bottle and set it aside. "How's things? You're good, Dad's good?"

They spoke for a few more minutes, catching up. Retirement was treating Dad very well; his golf game was better than ever. Mom had her book club, her volunteer hours at the library, her yoga class, the Historical Society. Mom and Dad played tennis twice a week at the club. His mom caught him up on the latest accomplishments of his niece and nephews. The usual. All was well.

By the time David left his office, it was just past ten o'clock. And he still wasn't tired. He felt restless, and didn't feel like heading back to his empty apartment just yet. Before he realized it, he was walking down Fifth Avenue... until he reached O'Reilly's Tavern. It was welcoming, an attractive and newer façade with wood and brass—a typical Irish bar.

For four nights now, since Sunday night, when he'd gotten into bed to go to sleep, the last thing he'd thought of was how Anna's lips had felt against his. How blue her eyes were. The wickedness in her grin. The sultry promise there.

It was time to take her up on those drinks she'd offered.

He pushed open the heavy door and was pelted by the cacophony of rock music and patrons' laughter and conversation. The bar was pretty crowded, but not stifling. As full as a decent bar in midtown Manhattan should be at ten on a Thursday night. David made his way further inside, assessing his surroundings. Polished wood, brass railing around a sturdy bar, a crowd varied in age and social status. Almost cozy.

Searching purposefully, his gaze landed on its target. There were two bartenders: a tall guy in his mid-forties, and Anna. She wore a tight black T-shirt, revealing tattoos on both arms. They weren't full sleeves, but there was quite a bit of ink. Her blonde hair was streaked with different colors now; she'd traded in the black and orange for... was it magenta or wine colored? He'd have to get closer to be sure. It was pulled back in a ponytail, which swayed as she grabbed a pint glass, pulled the lever on a tap, and filled it with amber liquid.

She hadn't been pulling his leg; she was a bartender. And she was there.

He watched her for two minutes, camouflaged in the crowd. She was quick and efficient as she worked, but didn't stop talking and had a dazzling smile for the people she spoke to. Her energy was palpable, a tangible presence.

She was so… different. Different from the women he usually met, usually talked to at parties, came into contact with at all. And without being able to explain why, he was drawn to her. Maybe it was because she was pretty and sexy; maybe because she was edgy and sassy; maybe it was because when she'd kissed him, something had flamed inside him that he hadn't been able to put out. He didn't know. He didn't care. He just knew he wanted to know more about her, and yes, kiss her again in the process.

He sidled past people until he got a spot at the bar on her side. When he caught her eye, her face lit up. Her thin brows lifted with surprise and she went to him.

"Well, well!" Her smile was wide and bright. "Look who we have here! My white knight in a suit!"

"Hardly," he said. "But yes, I'm here. I believe you offered me a drink."

"Was starting to think you'd never show." She grabbed a

square paper napkin and a cardboard coaster and placed them on the bar in front of him. Tossing him a smile, she asked, "What'll it be, David?"

She remembered his name. Satisfaction pierced him. He rested his elbows on the bar and asked, "Got any good scotch?"

"You bet your arse. Name it, we've got it."

"Laphroaig 10?"

"Sure. Ice, no ice?"

"None."

"That's a good man. Be right back."

He watched her as she moved, letting his eyes roam over her slender frame, all clad in black. Rock music pounded through the air; people talked around him. His eyes stayed glued to her as she reached for the Laphroaig, poured some into a glass, and set it before him.

"On me," she said with a grin. "I meant it. Your drinks tonight are on me."

"All night long," he reminded her.

Her gaze locked on his for a second, and her grin curved into something naughty. Flat-out sultry. "You can go all night long, David?"

Blood rushed south. *Damn.* He held her gaze as it heated, feeling that heat slowly burn through him as he nodded. His voice pitched low. "Absolutely."

She smiled. "Good to know."

"Annie!" A man's voice rang out from the end of the bar.

David turned to look as a dark-haired, bearded man in a dark wool peacoat raised a hand and called, "I'm goin' home. See ya tomorrow." He wrapped a black and red scarf around his neck.

"G'night, old man," she called back merrily with a quick wave. "Kiss the girls for me, tell Cass hi."

"Will do." The man turned and made his way to the door.

"Annie?" David asked curiously.

"Aye, he's always called me that." She huffed out a little laugh. "That's my brother, Sean."

Recall kicked in. "The one you followed to New York?"

She gave him an approving glance. "You have a good memory. Aye, that's him. He co-owns this bar with a friend of his."

"Ah." David nodded, then sipped his scotch. It went down nice and smooth.

"*Ah* what?" Anna asked.

David shrugged. "*Ah*, if he owns the bar, I guess that's how you ended up working here."

"Kind of. But there's a little more to it than just nepotism." Her gaze flickered to two men trying to get her attention to David's right. "Be back soon, Suit. Duty calls." She stepped away from him toward the other customers.

David loosened the knot of his tie and watched her. He wasn't going anywhere.

Chapter Three

"HOW LATE DO you work tonight?" David asked.

Anna grabbed a rag and wiped the wet spot on the bar beside him. "'Til midnight. Almost done with my shift."

She tried not to stare at him openly, but it was hard. David was a good-looking man, even in that expensive navy suit and tie. Maybe *especially* in that suit and tie. Which both confounded and amused her. She liked artists, creative types, tattooed bad boys... not white-collar frat boys.

David was from a different world. She hadn't thought he'd ever take her up on her offer and come into the bar. She knew men like him didn't give women like her the time of day. He looked slightly out of place here; he reeked of money and refinement and yes, power. But damn if there wasn't chemistry between them. All night, every time they held each other's gaze for more than a few seconds, electricity sizzled through her.

They made small talk in between her making and handling drinks. She found out he'd grown up in Short Hills, New Jersey, he now lived in the West Village, and was an investment banker for a prestigious firm in the city. He'd handed her his business card, and she recognized the firm; it was big-time. Which meant she'd been right: David Beren was big money, big business, high stakes... soooo not her type.

But she couldn't stop glancing at those full lips of his. She remembered very well that the kiss she'd planted on him had been returned... and had been scorching hot. Black lashes made his gorgeous hazel eyes stand out, a shade not too far off from the scotch he was sipping. And he was definitely sipping, not knocking them back. As if he wanted to draw out his time there, stay for a while. He'd walked in over an hour before, had asked her a bunch of questions about herself, and was now only finishing his second drink. Not a party boy, it seemed. There was an intense, focused vibe about him that she found compelling. Especially when it was aimed at her... and apparently, at the moment, it was. She caught the heated looks he kept tossing her way. It was interesting.

"You always work this late?" he asked when she returned to him again.

"Yup. I told you, five to midnight, and later on Saturdays if the bar's really full. We usually have two bartenders on weeknights for any shift, and three on Saturdays." She leaned in a bit, resting her hip against the bar. "Sean doesn't like me to stay 'til closing on Saturdays, which is two A.M. Says only dangerous characters are still out at that hour, and he worries about me. He wants me gone at midnight unless he really needs an extra hand."

"It's good that he watches out for you," David said.

"He does. Can't help himself." She chuckled. "I'm the seventh of eight kids. Someone was always watching out for me. It's both a comfort and a pain in the arse."

"*Eight* kids? Wow."

"Aye. You have any siblings?"

"Just one older brother. He's a cardiac surgeon. Lives on the Upper East Side, works out of Cornell."

"Well. That's impressive."

David gave a short nod. "So. Back to you. You keep vampire hours."

She laughed. "I do. But in bartending, the gigs are almost always at night, so it comes with the territory."

"You work gigs other than this one?"

"Sure, sometimes. A private party here and there—that's good, quick cash. And I spend my summers on Long Island. I hate being in the city during the summer. I need ocean air. I have a regular bartending gig down in Long Beach. I rent a room in a house with some friends and stay there from the middle of May to just past Labor Day."

His brows lifted. "Sweet. That sounds fun."

"It is."

He nodded slowly, and she could almost feel him filing away the information in his head. Something told her his sharp mind didn't miss a trick and held on to details.

She left him to serve another drink, then eventually made her way back to him, as she'd been doing since he got there. He picked up right where they'd left off.

"If you don't mind my asking," he said, "how old are you?"

She batted her eyes at him and teased, "A lady never tells."

"Oh, c'mon."

"Ha, no worries. I'm no lady." She winked. "I just turned thirty-one."

"You look maybe twenty-five," he said.

"Charmer."

"It's true and you know it." He grinned. "How long have you been a bartender?"

"Five years or so."

"You came all the way to New York to be a bartender?"

That made her pause. "Um. No. I came to New York because I'd always wanted to come here. So I went to school at FIT. I always loved fashion design…" She looked away, quickly scanning the scene to see if anyone needed a drink. "I went for a year and a half, then dropped out. But I had to do something if I wanted to stay in New York. Sean sent me to bartending school. So I'd have a job and be able to make decent money while I figured out what I wanted to do next."

David's eyes were so intense on her face, his gaze felt like heated beams. He radiated cool strength. She found herself drawn in.

"Okay," he said. "So… did you figure it out? What you wanted to do next?"

"No. Not yet. And that's fine." She shrugged. "Bartending is a good gig. The money's better than other jobs I'd get, considering I don't have a college degree. I make my own schedule. I wear what I want, meet a lot of people. I spend summers at the beach and the rest of the year in one of the best cities in the world. This works for me."

He nodded slowly and lifted his glass to his lips, finishing his drink.

She couldn't help but feel a twinge. He was surely judging her. Or maybe not. Either way, why did she care?

"Want another?" she asked as she took his empty glass.

He flicked a glance at his watch. A Rolex. Of course. "You're off in twenty minutes, you said?"

"If that means it's eleven-forty, then yes."

"Want to get something to eat when you're done with work?"

She stilled and stared at him. "Are you asking me out?"

"Yes." That gaze of his sucked her in, left her feeling a bit at his mercy.

And she liked that. It turned her on.

She blinked. So not her type. Different worlds. But something about him… "Sure," she said. "Why not? I could eat."

ANNA SIPPED HER beer slowly. She never drank until she was off the clock, and now that she was—and in the company of an attractive, attentive man—she definitely didn't want to get sloppy. Being a smart woman, she liked to stay sharp. This was her second, and would be her last, beer of the night.

She reached for one of the dwindling tortilla chips on the plate. The huge order of loaded nachos she and David had shared was almost gone. They'd both been hungry and demolished it in the hour they'd been tucked into a booth at Pancho's, a few blocks from the bar.

Small talk kept flowing, which was good. He'd surprised her. David was nicer than the growly bear she'd first encountered in the bakery, and definitely nicer than the obnoxious finance guys she was used to. Modest, even. If he had a big ego, he hid it well, because she didn't sense it. What he did have was a quiet, sure self-confidence that appealed to her more than she wanted to admit. He talked about himself and his life plainly, without bragging or trying to impress her or any swagger, and certainly not the whole *I'm better than you in every way* vibe she usually got from men like him.

And he *could* have bragged; the few details he'd told her about his career and background were impressive. But he didn't brandish those details—his fancy college education, the top-notch firm he worked for, his privileged upbringing—like swords to parry with. He just presented them as facts, and with some humble gratitude too. It was a refreshing surprise. She had to admit, she'd had him pegged differently.

She also loved the intensity of his hazel eyes. They drank her in; her words, her face, her body. Like he was downright thirsty. A man hadn't looked at her like that in a long time. It was a heady sensation.

She wondered if he was intense in bed, too.

"Have Yourself A Merry Little Christmas" came on over the sound system. David flicked a glance at the ceiling and rolled his eyes.

Anna couldn't help but laugh. "That was some look."

He snorted and reached for another chip. "It's only November first. It's just a little early for Christmas music, don't you think?"

"Nah, I love it." She grabbed another chip and scooped some chopped tomato onto it. "I gather you don't?"

"You gather incorrectly. I don't mind Christmas music," he clarified. "I just mind it being rammed down my throat the second Halloween is over. To me, the holiday season shouldn't start until the day after Thanksgiving." He wiped his fingers with a napkin. "When Santa Claus comes down the street at the end of the Macy's Thanksgiving parade? *That* is the official start of the holiday season."

"Yeah, well, most people don't agree with you anymore on that."

"I've noticed." He shook his head and added, "Commercialism took over the holidays. Like everything else."

She nudged his forearm with her fingers. "Oh c'mon, David. Where's your Christmas spirit?"

He grasped his beer and said, "I don't have any."

"What?" She stared at him. "That's awful! You're a Grinch, are ya?"

"No. I'm Jewish." He took a sip.

"Oh." That wasn't the response she'd been expecting.

His brows furrowed. "Is there a problem?"

She noted the sudden harder edge to his voice and said quickly, "What, that you're Jewish? Of course not. You just caught me by surprise with that answer. Thought you were either kidding around, or just being a Grinch."

He nodded and set down his glass. "I like the holiday season in general, but yeah, it's a little different for me."

"Annoying?"

"Excuse me?"

"I've always thought it must be annoying to those who don't celebrate Christmas, being bombarded by it everywhere if it's not your deal."

"Interesting that you think of that at all. A lot of people don't." The corners of his mouth ticked up. "It doesn't bother me, actually. It's just how the world is. I don't really pay it any mind." He grabbed a chip and dipped it in what was left of the guacamole.

"Well," Anna said, "I have to admit, I know very little about Hanukkah. Just the basics."

"The basics?" David's hint of a bemused grin turned into

a full-blown smile. "And what are those? I'm curious to hear. Enlighten me."

She smiled back. "Hey, I've lived in New York for over seven years. You can't *not* pick up things about Judaism if you live here, unless you go out of your way not to. I'm a lot of things, but I'm not an arsehole."

A chuckle burst from him. "True. The city is wonderfully diverse." He slanted her a playful look. "So? The basics? I'm waiting."

"I know there are eight nights," she began. "Which, if you ask me, is a hella sweet deal. Eight nights of presents instead of one? You guys win on that."

"We certainly do. What else?"

"You light a candle and say a prayer every night of Hanukkah. There are eight candles but a big one in the middle, and the candle holder is called a menorah."

"Very good. Bonus point for knowing there's a different one in the middle. What else?"

She shrugged and admitted, "That's it. That's all I know."

"Okay. Well, I suppose those *are* the crucial basics. You've got the essential things down." He tipped his beer in her direction. "Not bad."

"So tell me more," she said, leaning in. "Your turn to enlighten me."

His eyes seemed to glow as he regarded her. "What do you want to know?"

"Why is the middle candle bigger than the others? Is it a symbol of something?"

"Excellent question. It's because you light that middle one first, then use that candle to light the others. It has a name; it's called the *shamash*."

"Cool," she said, nodding. "Okay."

"What else do you want to know?"

"Are you very religious?"

"Me?" His eyes widened and he huffed out a short laugh. "Noooo. I'm what you'd call a very relaxed Jew."

She giggled.

"I was bar mitzvahed," he added, "but that was about it. I mean..." He stole a quick sip of beer. "Now I have a question. Do you go to church every Sunday?"

She barked out a laugh. "Heavens, no."

"But you consider yourself Catholic, that's how you were raised, right?" He held up a hand. "Not to make assumptions, but if you're Irish, that's a pretty good bet."

"Aye, you're right. On both counts."

"Well, it's the same for me. I'm Jewish, but I don't go to temple. My parents only go on the High Holidays; I don't even do that. You don't have to go to your place of worship every week to be what you are. You are what you are. Or what you want to be." He shrugged. "That's how I see it, anyway."

"I feel the same," Anna said. "Exactly the same."

"Cool." He leaned in and slanted her a look. "Now I'm

curious. Have you ever dated a Jewish guy before?"

"No. Kissed a few, though."

"Ha! I bet you have."

"What?" She leaned in too. "What does that mean?"

"It means you're gorgeous," he said intently, "so you can probably kiss any man you decide to."

Her heart gave a little skip. "Ya think so?"

"Yup."

Their eyes locked as the air became charged between them.

Anna swallowed hard, willing her heart to slow down. Whispers in the back of her mind helped her to keep her cool. Christopher's voice, and the flat hardness of his pale blue eyes… "Guys like you don't go for girls like me," she finally said, slowly leaning back in her seat.

"What? Says who?" David demanded.

"Says my personal experience. And most of your colleagues, I'd bet."

"Well, screw my colleagues, then."

"Ha! You bring women bartenders with tattoos to your golf outings, do ya?" She fixed him with a sharp look. "Or to the country club? Or your fancy office parties?"

He met her gaze with a steely one of his own. "You watch too many movies."

"Nope. I *work* those parties, Suit." She didn't break eye contact. "I'm the woman behind the bar at all those places, and I see guys like you. And I'm invisible to you. Except for a few that feel like getting wild, going out of their lane and taking a walk on the wild side for a night. They hit on me like they're entitled to a piece of me, and they're always creeps." She reached for her beer. It was almost empty. "*You're* not a creep, but I'm right about this. And you know it."

He just stared harder, his dark eyes drilling through her. "Maybe. I'm not going to discount your experiences. I'm sure they're based in fact. But I'm not that guy."

She drank her beer, knocking back the rest until it was finished. "If you say so."

"I do." David pressed on. "What kind of guy am I, then? Hit me."

"To the naked eye? A privileged, rich, fast-living, power-hungry finance guy." Something in her whispered that might not be true, but she stood her ground.

"Well, that's wrong." His jaw set tightly, but his voice stayed calm. "I grew up with privilege, and I'm not denying that. Hell, I just *told* you about that. But I don't feel entitled to anything, and I never have. I've worked damn hard to get where I am. I'm not rich, but yes, I do well. I don't live the fast life these days, not like I did in my twenties. That lost its appeal years ago." His voice pitched lower. "And the only thing I'm hungry for right now is *you*."

Oh holy hell. Anna's blood rushed through her body. "Is that so?" she said as casually as she could.

"Yup." He didn't move, didn't blink, and his intense

gaze melted her. "You're fierce."

"Sometimes."

"I bet all the time."

She shrugged. She hoped her air of cavalier nonchalance didn't give away how her heart was beating too fast and her blood felt like fire under her skin.

"Let's get out of here," he said.

Shock wobbled through her and she huffed out a dry laugh. "Pretty bold, aren't you?"

"Yes. And so are you," he said, his voice low and sure. "You're bold and fierce and vibrant and fun. And unbearably hot. Gorgeous. And at the very least, I want to kiss you again. See if a second kiss would be even hotter than the first one. But I'm not kissing you in the middle of this restaurant."

Whoa. She licked her lips, and noticed his eyes tracked the motion. "Umm…"

"Anna. I might sound like a bit of a caveman at this moment, but I'm not an axe murderer or anything." He reached across the table and took her hand, wrapping his warm fingers around hers. The contact sent a little zing through her. "Should I get you some references?"

She laughed. "At this time of night? That'd be something."

"But I could if you wanted."

"Something tells me you're probably right about that."

His fingers stroked hers gently as they stared at each other. "I'm not trying to be pushy, or demanding. I'm not asking you to go home with me. I just want to kiss you again. That's all."

"Is that all?"

"I'd be lying if I said no. But let's just take a walk." His other hand came up, warmly enveloping hers between both of his. "How about that? Out in public, so you feel safe. Would that be okay?"

"Yes," she said.

Before she knew it, they were walking down Fifth Avenue, hand in hand. At first, they were silent, the anticipation and chemistry threatening to choke them both. Then David asked her how Christmas in New York was compared to Christmas in Ireland.

"They're different animals," she said, and he laughed. "Everything here is bigger, louder, and brighter." As if to cement her point, she waved her free hand around at all the surrounding buildings, blaring with light and sound.

"Do you go back to Ireland for Christmas?" he asked.

"I used to go almost every year," she said. A cold breeze blew, making her hair dance around her face. Winter was definitely around the corner. She shoved her free hand into the pocket of her puffy silver coat. "I've a huge family, and it's nice to see everyone. But last year, I didn't. Because Sean and his wife had a new baby, their second. They have two girls, and I adore them. I stayed here to be with them."

"That must've been nice," David said.

"It was," Anna said. "Cassandra—that's my sister-in-law—is from Long Island. Her family is there, and her extended family, and they throw a huge gathering on Christmas Eve. Like, forty people. So Sean and Cass brought me along. It was just as loud and fun as a McKinnon Christmas back home, but with better food. Cass's Italian mom and aunt cook up a storm."

"Sounds fantastic," David said with a little smile.

She peered at him and asked, "What do you do on Christmas? You don't have to work, right?"

"Work? The whole world is closed. I couldn't work if I wanted to."

"So what do you do?"

"Enjoy the day off. Some years, I've been invited to friends' homes for Christmas dinner. Some years, I just do the stereotypical Jewish Christmas."

"And what's that?" she asked, genuinely curious.

"You don't know?" His lips quirked up in a wry smile. "Go out for Chinese food and then go to the movies. Those are the only two things open on Christmas."

She laughed. "I see. So that's a Jewish Christmas, huh?"

"Yup. And I also usually catch up on work at home. It's a good day for that, since the world is so quiet."

"West Village is home, you said?" she asked.

"Yes."

"Aha. That's why I ran into you at the bakery."

"You didn't run into me. You punched me in the face,

36

though."

She blushed a bit, thankful for the cover of night to hide it. "I said I was sorry."

"I'm not sorry," he said. "I'm glad you did, actually."

"What? You're putting me on."

"No, I am. Because we met."

A pleased smile bloomed across her face.

"I was totally checking you out from behind," he admitted. "But I probably wouldn't have said a word to you. You did me a favor."

"Then I don't have to apologize again. What a relief."

He smiled back. "Where do you live? You wouldn't say before."

"East Village."

"Doesn't surprise me. So what were you doing at the bakery?"

"Sean, Cass, and the girls live in the West Village. I was on my way to see them. The cupcakes were for my nieces."

"You're a doting auntie."

"Blatantly in love with them," she declared.

"Where do they live?"

"West 13th and Seventh."

David chuckled. "That's funny. They're around the corner from me."

"Shut up!" Anna exclaimed. "Seriously?"

"Practically. I'm on West 11th and Sixth."

"Oh my God." She let out a bemused chuckle too.

"That's… bizarre."

"That bakery has the best cinnamon rolls going. That's why I was there."

"I'll have to go back and try one."

"I'll take you there, if you like."

She couldn't wipe the smile off her face. She felt giddy. "You know, I'd never set foot in there until that day. Walked by it a million times, but never went in before."

His eyes set intently on her face. "*Bashert,*" he murmured.

"What?"

"It's a Yiddish word," he explained. "It means 'destiny'." He stopped walking, causing her to stop too. He gazed at her for a few charged moments, then cradled her face in his hands and pressed his mouth to hers.

Chapter Four

ANNA OPENED HER eyes halfway, disoriented. She didn't recognize the room she was in. A tilt of her head to see David next to her, naked and asleep, brought it all rushing back. Swallowing a groan, she licked her dry lips and stared at him. Damn, he was gorgeous. Dark, heavy stubble covered his strong jaw, and his thick hair was adorably rumpled. His shoulders and arms were somewhat defined; not bulging with muscles, but sculpted enough to appeal to her. She reached out and lightly touched the dark hair on his chest. He had a lean, taut build that she'd very much enjoyed last night.

All night.

She'd gone home with him and they'd been all over each other until almost dawn.

She hadn't done anything this spontaneous or reckless or impulsive in a long time. Anna wanted to berate herself... but the night had been too damn good. She wasn't sorry. He wasn't an axe murderer; he was a sex beast. And, when he hadn't been rocking her world over and over, he'd been a total gentleman. Making sure she was comfortable, bringing her water to drink in bed, whispering compliments in her ear…

His full lips were parted in sleep. God, what he'd done to her with that mouth last night. His breathing was a little heavy, but he wasn't snoring. Of course he didn't snore, he was too refined for that. She wanted to lick him awake. But… deep down, she knew that when he woke up, he'd likely see the tattooed girl in his bed and recoil.

The thought of that made Anna's stomach clench.

Maybe she wasn't being fair. He hadn't treated her with anything but respect. From the very start, when as soon as the door to his apartment closed and he pushed her back against the wall to kiss her, he'd paused to say, "Is this okay? You're good with this?"

But, as she'd experienced before, men could see things differently in the light of day. And the thought of him being anything other than that sweet, sexy, openly lusty guy she'd spent the night with made her heart twist in her chest.

Now, with sunshine streaming through the blinds, she looked around his bedroom. Small, neat, masculine. White walls, a tiny desk in the corner with his laptop and a stack of papers on top, the one window. One dark wood dresser. The dark brown comforter on his queen-sized bed was soft and unbelievably plush.

She remembered how they kissed like teenagers in the elevator of his building the night before, up the six floors to his apartment. She'd been both breathless and a little nervous by the time she got to his door, but refused to show it. He'd turned to smile at her and said, "Last chance to change your mind. Because I really want you."

She'd all but pounced on him.

David let out the tiniest snore, breaking Anna out of her reverie. He rolled away from her, onto his side.

Carefully, as stealthy as a cat burglar, Anna climbed out of bed. A glance at the tiny digital clock on his nightstand told her it was only 7:34. So she'd gotten, what, maybe three hours of sleep? God, what a night… memories flooded her as she stood there and gazed down at him.

He'd been a lot of fun. So damn hot. And sweet. Sweeter than any alpha male had a right to be during a one-night stand.

Then she turned away. She had to.

Her panties were across the room, along with her bra. Tiptoeing out of the bedroom, she located her shirt and leggings in the living room. As she got dressed, she wondered if she should leave a note. But what would she say?

She grabbed her bag and went into the bathroom. She'd noticed last night that it wasn't typical of a bachelor; like the rest of the apartment, it was clean and tidy. David, unlike a lot of men she'd known, was neat and orderly. That made her smile for some reason. Finding mouthwash under the sink—*praise all that was holy*—she rinsed her mouth out, washed her hands, then pulled her tangled mess of hair into a ponytail. She wet a tissue and dabbed away the smudged mascara beneath her eyes, found her fuchsia lipstick in her bag and applied it, and checked her appearance one last time.

Oh crap. *Crap.* David had marked her. There was a dark bruise on her neck, just below her ear. Recalling how he'd given her that made her shiver. She took down the ponytail and tried to cover the hickey with her hair. The cover-up stick in her makeup case helped, but it was still visible. Just great. Ah well.

She slipped out of the apartment in careful silence.

As she emerged onto the street, the morning sun slapped her in the face. Groaning, she foraged through her bag for her sunglasses and put them on with a sigh of relief, then walked to the corner to hail a cab. There were yellow taxis everywhere, and she didn't have the patience to call an Uber. Getting across town would be hard at this time of morning, with rush hour traffic, but she wasn't up for the walk. All she wanted was to fall into her own bed and sleep the rest of the morning away. Then, coffee and a shower, and something to eat, and maybe more sleep until she had to go to work.

But first, she sent a text to David. She couldn't just leave without a word. She'd have hated it if he'd done it to her, so she wouldn't do it to him. She pulled out the business card he'd given her with his cell number on it.

Thank you for a memorable evening, she typed into her phone. *And for not being an axe murderer. ~Anna*

Okay. Done. She lifted her hand to hail a cab.

"Annie?" said a familiar male voice behind her. A baby

squealed happily.

She cringed. *Shit.* Shit shit shit. She turned to face her brother. "Hey, Sean."

"Well, good mornin'!" He stood behind the stroller, looking her over as Ella shrieked in delight and kicked her feet at seeing her beloved aunt.

"Hi there, baby girl," Anna cooed, crouching down to give her niece kisses and hugs. Squirming excitedly, the baby babbled and put her tiny hands on Anna's cheeks. "Oh, you wee sweet thing. It's so nice to see you!"

"It's nice to see you too," Sean said from above her. "So unexpected. What are you doin' on this side of town? At this early hour, no less?"

As she rose to stand up and face him, his eyes narrowed shrewdly.

"Um..." She shrugged. His blue eyes shot to her neck. She moved her hair to cover the mark but knew she was too late.

"Doin' the walk of shame, it looks like," he said with a laugh. Crossing his arms over his chest, he smirked. "Am I right?"

"Shut up, Sean," she muttered. "Why are you even here?"

"I just dropped Rose at school. We live nearby... *as you know.* Coincidence, huh?" He swallowed a laugh, and she wanted to kick him. "Was goin' to get some breakfast at the bagel place before we went back home." The amused smirk stayed. "Care to join us?"

Her stomach growled and Ella kept making sweet babble noises, but Anna said, "Can I take a rain check? I just want to go home and get some sleep."

"I bet. Long night, eh?"

"Knock it off, ya smug bastard."

Sean laughed. "Ah, Annie. Should I ask if you were safe?"

"You should ask me nothing. It's none of your business."

The smirk finally faded. "True. But that doesn't mean I don't worry when I see you like this. A lot of men are—"

"It was fine, and I'm fine. He's a good guy." At least, she'd trusted him enough to go home with him. Her gut rarely steered her wrong. But Sean's brotherly concern made her wince a bit. He was right. It wasn't the smartest thing she'd ever done; she didn't know David well. "I know," she said, holding up a hand to cut the words from Sean's mouth. "*I know.* But… thank you for caring."

"I always care." The corner of his mouth quirked up. "And I'll always tease you too. Big brother rights."

"We're too old for that shite," she said.

"Ah, never, Annie. No time limits on that one."

She gave him a quick kiss on the cheek, crouched down to hug Ella, then turned back to the street and raised her hand for a cab. Mercifully, a yellow taxi slid right over to stop in front of her.

Sean opened the door for her and tossed her a wink. "Get some sleep, missy. See you tonight."

Anna gave the driver her address and sank down in the seat. Of all people to catch her doing the walk of shame, did it have to be her brother? Sweet Jesus, that was just her luck.

ANNA WAS DISTRACTED at work that night. She couldn't shake the memory of her incredibly hot night with David. When she'd woken up at two in the afternoon, there'd been a text waiting for her.

David: *Thanks for letting me know you're okay.*

That had been it.

She didn't know why it made her feel bad. He hadn't berated her, or trashed the fact that she'd snuck out without a goodbye. But the text was perfunctory. It made her uneasy. Like she'd done something wrong.

Protecting herself wasn't wrong.

"Anna?" John's voice broke through. The other bartender working with her tonight, he'd been there longer than Sean had, from back when Jimmy O'Reilly first opened the bar over a decade before. "You're a little off tonight."

"I know," she said. "Sorry."

"You okay?"

"Yeah. Just tired… and a little preoccupied."

"I noticed." John winked at her and reached past her for a pint glass. As he filled it with Sam Adams at the tap, he said, "Need anything?"

"No, I'm fine, really." She smiled warmly at him. The tall, burly guy was like another older brother. "Thanks, though."

The bar was crowded tonight, which she was thankful for. Being busy made it hard to get lost in her thoughts. Hard to wonder what David thought of her, and their night together. Or to think about how sinfully delicious it had been to rip him out of his suit. To tear off his blazer and let it drop to the floor, to pull off his tie and toss it across the living room, to unbutton that crisp white shirt and reach for his belt buckle and the way he'd groaned deep when she—

"Dammit, girl," she muttered to herself. "Get your head outta your arse."

By ten, the bar was packed. The music was loud, and the lively buzz of voices and laughter even louder. Anna liked when the place went into full swing. That energy was a tangible thing, and it often carried her through the hours, making a night go quickly. Working up a sweat, she was dying to put her hair up in a ponytail, but couldn't. In her mind, she cursed David yet again for leaving that mark.

And as if he'd heard her, he pushed through the other patrons to plant himself at the bar, right in front of her. In another dark suit and tie, looking calm and sexy, all he said was, "Hey."

Her stomach did a wobbly flip. "Hey."

Their eyes locked for a few seconds. He leaned his elbows on the bar. Her heart felt fluttery in her chest and she swallowed hard. She really hadn't thought she'd ever see him again. Then she slapped down a paper napkin in front of him and said, "What'll it be?"

"Any IPA," he said. "Surprise me." His stare went to her neck, and his eyes sparkled with triumph.

Oh damn him. No way would she show him anything but a cool and collected front. Switching out the paper napkin for a cardboard coaster, she gave a curt nod, a bright smile, and said, "IPA, comin' up."

Why is he here? The question ran through her mind over and over as she tried to look casual. She filled a glass with Julius and set it in front of him. "Here you go. Think you'll like this one."

He only arched a heavy brow at her before taking a sip. As soon as he did, he asked, "Julius?"

"Aye. You know your IPAs."

"It's my favorite, actually."

She nodded again and went to move away when he asked, "You okay?"

"Fine," she said brightly.

"Honestly, Anna?"

The note of earnestness in his deep voice stopped her. She met his gaze. "Yes."

The few seconds that stretched out felt like forever.

Then he said, "Okay. Good." He took a large gulp, then pulled out his wallet and dropped a ten-dollar bill on the bar. "See you."

She watched him walk out of the bar and wondered what that had been about. Was he just checking to see if she was okay? Had he been hoping she'd say something to give him an opening so they could see each other again? Was he just making a point that she wasn't getting?

She had no idea. But most of all, she wondered if she'd made a mistake by letting him walk out of the bar.

Chapter Five

ALL THE NEXT day, Anna buzzed. She felt the restless hum in her head, under her skin, simmering in her blood. Why had David come to the bar? What was he after? She couldn't figure it out, and she couldn't shake him out of her system.

She hadn't heard from him again. Maybe she never would. And she didn't know if that was a good thing or a bad thing.

By the time she got to work that evening, she was wired and on edge.

"Hey, lady!" Cassandra was sitting at the bar, and hopped off her stool to give her sister-in-law a big hug.

"What are you doing here?" Anna asked. "You rarely visit us."

"Sean and I have tickets to a show," Cassandra said. "We got a sitter for the girls. We're having a date night."

"Well, isn't that nice." Anna smiled as she and Cass headed to the back. Anna always left her coat and bag safely locked in Sean and Jimmy's office. When she opened the door, Sean held up a finger to them as he snarled into the phone, "No, mate, I ordered *fourteen* cases of that. You sent me *four*. So yeah, I'd say we have a problem."

"Oh boy," Cassandra murmured. Anna quickly stowed her stuff away and the women left the office. "That didn't sound good."

"It happens," Anna said. "Sean handles it. No worries."

"He said he had some business to wrap up before we went to dinner," Cass said. "That's why I was waiting out front." She slipped her arm through Anna's and slanted a catlike smile. "That, and I wanted to see you."

"You did, eh?" Anna asked.

"Yes." Cassandra's dark eyes absolutely twinkled as she added, "Wanted to ask you something about a walk of shame?"

Anna had to laugh, even as she shook her head in disdain. "Sean needs to keep his damn mouth shut."

"He tells me everything," Cassandra said as Anna untangled her arm and slipped behind the bar.

"Hey, Johnny," Anna greeted her co-worker, giving him a quick peck on the cheek.

"Hey, girl." John looked to Cassandra and asked, "Another Chardonnay?"

"No thank you," Cass said. "I'm here to have some girl talk with my favorite sister-in-law before Sean and I leave."

"That's my cue to get scarce, then." John grinned at them before walking to the other side of the bar.

Anna leaned against the bar to get closer to her. "Cass,

listen."

"No, *you* listen," Cassandra said, cutting her off. "Sean tells me everything. What he told me, that he didn't tell you, is he was worried about you."

Anna rolled her eyes, leaned on her elbows, and huffed out a frustrated sigh. "I'm a grown woman, fer Chrissakes."

"I know. I told him the same thing." Cass leaned in more to drop her voice. "So… got stuff to tell me? Want to talk?"

Anna opened her mouth to say no. But suddenly realized… maybe she did.

She and Cassandra were close. Cass was so smart, intuitive, and trustworthy. And, like Anna, Cass was always brutally honest. All these qualities made her a good sounding board.

"Can you not tell Sean whatever I tell you?" Anna asked. "Coz the truth is… maybe I could use a drop of… feedback."

"You mean advice," Cassandra corrected her. "You're as stubborn as your brother, not wanting to admit something like that." She covered Anna's hands with her own, her warm brown eyes pinning her. "Honey. Talk to me."

Anna spilled the short tale of her experience with David, up to his brief appearance the night before at the bar.

"Sounds to me like he was just checking on you," Cassandra offered. "You pulled a disappearing act, he doesn't know you well, and he wanted to make sure you were all right."

"But why?" Anna asked in exasperation. "Why would he come all the way over here to do that, only to turn around and leave?"

"You tell me."

Anna stared at her blankly.

"From what you just told me, you didn't even throw him any crumbs."

"What do you mean?"

"Did you give him any indication you wanted to see him again?" Cassandra asked. "Were you inviting, or flirty, or even just *nice* to him?"

"Um… no, not really."

"Well, men have pride. If he didn't think you were open to that, maybe once he saw you were truly okay, and that you didn't want anything more from him, he figured he'd cut his losses."

"But I…" Anna swallowed. *But I do want to see him again* is what almost flew out of her mouth. Without any forethought, that had been her unfiltered reaction. She bit down on her lip as she pondered that.

"Do you want to see him again?" Cassandra asked, as if she'd read her mind.

Anna only shrugged, unwilling to admit that she did.

Cassandra laughed. "God! Well, you keep that up. Good luck with that."

"He's an *investment banker*," Anna said, as if that ex-plained everything.

"And?"

"And…" Anna shrugged again, not knowing how to say what she was thinking without it sounding pathetic. She grabbed a rag from beneath the bar and started rubbing the polished mahogany.

Cassandra's hand shot out to grasp Anna's wrist, stopping her and forcing her to look up. "Anna. You're one of the most fearless women I've ever met. What are you scared of with this guy?"

Anna's mouth went dry. "I'm not scared."

"Bullshit. I know you, remember? It's all over your face." Cassandra's hand moved up her wrist to her fingers to give them a squeeze. "*Talk*, for Pete's sake."

Anna snorted, but then sighed. "I could… I could fall for a guy like him," she said. "There, I said it."

"And you're afraid it won't be mutual."

"*He's an investment banker*," Anna repeated, as if she were trying to make Cassandra understand a foreign language. "For one of the best firms around. I'm a bartender. Men like him sleep with women like me; they don't *date* women like me."

Cassandra's jaw actually dropped open before she snapped, "That's an awful thing to say. You're smart, strong, and flipping gorgeous."

"You're not hearing me," Anna said.

"Oh, I heard you. I just hate what I heard."

"Doesn't make it any less true," Anna murmured, looking away. "Trust me on that." She grabbed a rag and rubbed at a spot on the bar as she said under her breath, "I've got personal experience on that."

"Maybe he's not all men, he's just him," Cassandra pressed on. "And maybe he likes you and wants to see you again, but you offered zero encouragement."

Anna frowned as she took that in.

"You want to see him again?" Cassandra asked.

"Maybe."

"Did you tell him that?"

"No."

"Well, maybe you should." Now it was Cassandra who rolled her eyes. "Clue him in, and see what happens. Maybe he's a jerk. But maybe he's not. Only one way to find out. *Duh.*"

Anna laughed, her tension broken. "Don't ever hold back, Cass."

"Not in this lifetime, girl."

DAVID STRETCHED HIS arm back, then let out a Serena-worthy grunt as he served the ball. Mike volleyed it back, and David went after it. Sweat poured down his forehead and dripped down his back as he played. His laser-like focus and determination extended to all things, and tennis had always been high on that list.

By the time the third match was done, Mike had lost all

three.

"You're lucky I like you," Mike said when they finished. Both panting and sweating, they leaned against the wall as David handed his longtime friend a bottle of water. "You thrashed me today. Holy crap."

"Felt good," David said between breaths.

"Screw you," Mike said on a laugh.

They put down their racquets, worked to catch their breath and gulped down water. The sounds of other matches still going on around them at the indoor tennis club echoed off the high walls.

Mike shot his friend a sideways glance. "You played like you were trying out for the Olympics or something. Harder than usual. What's going on with you?"

"Just needed a good workout," David said before finishing off his bottle. He tossed it into a nearby blue recycling can.

"If you say so." Mike finished his water too and sent the empty bottle sailing through the air into the can. "Three points!"

"That's the only thing you won."

"Dude. What crawled up your ass and died today?"

David shook his head. "Just... stuff."

"I should've known you had something going on when you asked to play this early on a Sunday. I should be home telling my wife to let me sleep."

"If you'd stayed home, you should be helping your wife

take care of the baby and letting *her* sleep."

Mike gaped. "What the fuck is up with you?"

David pushed off the wall. "That… was really rude. Sorry."

"Talk, Dave. Go on."

"Don't want to talk about it. I'm just a dick today. It's not you."

"Oh, I knew that," Mike said with a good-natured laugh. He clapped a hand on David's shoulder. "Whatever it is, hope kicking my ass this morning helped a little."

David sighed. Mike Ferrell had been one of his closest friends since their undergrad days. They'd both gotten jobs in the city, been through it all together. Now married with a kid and living on the Upper West Side, they didn't see each other as much. But David trusted Mike like few others; Mike knew him so well. It was why he'd reached out to see him in the first place. "Thanks for coming. And tell Brittany I said thanks for letting you come out to play."

"Yeah, well," Mike said, "between work and now with the baby, I never see you anymore. I don't see *anyone* anymore, other than family. She knows that, and she was fine with it. Plus, it's not like you wanted to do a bar crawl. It's tennis on a Sunday morning." Mike gave his slightly bulging belly a disdainful glare. "Secretly, I think she wants me to battle the slowly encroaching Dad Bod I've got going on. And so do I."

They chuckled as they grabbed their towels and racquets.

"Then we should do this once a month, at least," David suggested.

"I'd be down for that," Mike said as they walked off the court. "If you can bring Dave my friend next time and not Dave the asshole."

"I can do that."

As he showered, David thought over Mike's words. Yes, he'd played ferociously. It was a way to burn off his frustration. Since he'd woken up on Friday morning to an empty bed, he hadn't been able to get Anna McKinnon off his mind.

He was a man who was used to getting what he wanted, and wasn't afraid of the hard work it took to get it. His fierce drive and dogged determination were two of his strongest traits, and he was proud of that. He'd accomplished many things with those tools in his basket.

And he'd had one-night stands. More than a few. He hadn't minded a bit when other women dropped off his radar, or when he walked away from some of them.

So why was Anna under his skin like this?

He let the water beat down on his scalp, his neck, and shoulders as she went through his mind yet again. She was barely contained fire in a soft, pretty package. Her skin had felt like velvet under his hands. The colorful tattoos on her body intrigued him, and yes, they only made her more sexy and alluring, if that was possible.

Sexy... she was the sexiest woman he'd been with in a

long time. Maybe ever, if he was honest. The way her breath caught and the lusty moan she'd let out when he pushed into her for the first time made him shudder with desire every time he recalled them. She'd wrapped herself around him and he'd lost himself in her.

Sex was always good, sure. It was pretty hard to have bad sex with someone. But with her, everything had been goddamned electric. Off the charts heat level. And they'd gone at it all night, unable to keep their hands off each other. The way she felt, smelled, sounded, the things she did to him...

He was hard now just thinking about it.

But it wasn't just that. In between rounds, it had been... nice. Easy. Even something akin to comfortable. He'd made sure she felt safe there. He wasn't used to bringing strange women home, and nowadays more than ever, he wanted her to feel safe and secure in his home and in his presence. He'd done everything he knew how to make her feel that way. And she'd seemed to get that, or he'd thought she did. They'd talked about things that didn't matter much: movies they'd seen and liked, different kinds of scotch, stories of rowdy or memorable customers in the bar. Not business, not banking, not financial statements or company politics or anything related to his work, which had been such a damn relief. It had been a fun night. He had fallen asleep feeling content and smiling, not thinking about work for the first time in forever.

Which was why it'd bothered him so much to wake up and find her gone.

At least she'd texted him, hadn't just vanished without a word, but still. It stung.

Plus, he'd been late for work because he'd overslept on a Friday morning. He *never* did that.

The whole damn thing was bizarre, for several reasons. It had been totally out of character for him. First and foremost, to put it simply, Anna wasn't his type. He usually went out with refined brunettes who had multiple degrees and talked about tax brackets or used legalese, not tattooed blondes who tended bar and swore like a sailor. He never brought a woman he barely knew back to his place. And he certainly didn't have the intense, wild sex they'd enjoyed all night.

But Anna was smart. And she was also something the women he usually dated weren't: funny. She had a quick, sharp sense of humor, and was sassy to boot. And as strong as any of the women he worked with, but Anna wasn't... tough. Not jaded or cynical. He'd seen hints of her sweetness. And yes, that she was gorgeous and sexy was absolutely a bonus.

And she apparently wanted nothing more to do with him. That was something he wasn't used to. He had to admit, his ego was bruised.

Damn. He wasn't a millionaire, but he lived well and had plenty of things to offer. And yeah, women usually liked those perks. Anna, it seemed, didn't give a crap. Which amused and intrigued him, but also frustrated him. She'd been with him solely because of the incredible chemistry between them. Plain sexual spark. She couldn't deny it any more than he could, and they'd gone with it.

She was a bartender, for Pete's sake. He knew she didn't care that he was Jewish and she was Catholic—that had absolutely zero to do with it. It was the other differences that likely had made her vanish. The different worlds thing. She probably usually went for huge, muscled guys with more tattoos than she had. Or creative types, or just... not the guy he knew she'd initially thought he was. What had she said? *A privileged, rich, fast-living, power-hungry finance guy.* He'd hoped he'd shown her, at least somewhat in the hours they'd spent together, that he was *not* that guy, dammit.

And he'd seen glimpses of softness underneath her savvy that had affected him more than he'd wanted to cop to. How, when in his arms, she'd relaxed, looked deep into his eyes and gave these sweet little smiles that did funny things to his gut. She'd bathed in the quiet, almost tender moments like a flower soaked up sunlight.

The truth was, so had he.

As he toweled off and dressed in the locker room, David thought, yet again, about how he'd felt compelled to go see her at her bar that night even though she'd clearly blown him off, and how aloof she'd been. Yes, he'd shown up on her turf without warning, but he wanted to make sure she was truly okay. He wanted to see if the connection he'd thought might be there was really there. And he'd felt that jolt of electricity when their eyes locked... but she'd given him nothing. She'd chosen his favorite IPA; a strange coincidence he'd love to take as a sign, but she had walls up. He saw them clear as day. And that night, still nursing the sting of her leaving, he just didn't have it in him to scale them.

If she didn't want to see him again, he'd thought, fine. So be it.

But he'd burned with frustration since the moment he'd walked out of the bar. And that she'd let him.

Now he had to decide if he'd pursue her or not. He had little interest in pursuing someone who didn't want to be pursued. His life was too busy to play games, or to invest time and energy on a woman who wasn't interested.

"Damn," he murmured, swallowing a sigh. Pulling on jeans, his old Cornell sweatshirt, and sneakers, he willfully shook her out of his head.

When he and Mike parted ways in front of the building, he squinted up at the sky. It was a blustery, overcast Sunday. A quick look at his phone showed him it was noon.

He ran his errands. Dry cleaners, food shopping. Made a quick call to his parents to say hello. By the time he got back to his apartment, it was almost four o'clock. Thanks to the time change, it'd be dark in about an hour. David hated that, and he wasn't good with being idle. He needed to always be doing something. But he had no plans for the rest of the evening. He grabbed his laptop and sat on his couch to rake through emails.

The buzzer from the concierge on the intercom went off.

He frowned as he looked at it from across the room. He wasn't expecting anyone. Probably someone hitting his buzzer by accident. Ignoring it, he reached for his reading glasses and put them on.

The buzzer went off again.

With an annoyed sigh, he got up and went to the intercom. "Hello?"

"You have a delivery," came the doorman's voice. The intercom always made voices sound tinny and fuzzy, like a drive-through fast food window.

"I didn't order anything," he said. "Must be a mistake."

"Yet here I am," said a woman's voice, "with a special delivery for David Beren."

The voice had a distinctly lyrical lilt. An Irish lilt. His blood surged through his entire body. "I'll be down in a minute." He took off his reading glasses, placed them on the small table by the door, snatched up his keys, and dashed out.

In the elevator, he ran his fingers through his hair as his heart thumped. Anna had come to see him. He couldn't have been any more shocked than he was. Anticipation, excitement, and something like hope all rushed through his veins.

When the doors of the elevator slid apart, he saw Anna standing at the small concierge booth, chatting with George, the doorman on duty. She wore jeans, an olive-colored jacket, and a hot pink and orange scarf—the colors weren't too different from the dyed streaks in her blonde hair, which hung loosely around her shoulders. She held a fat white box in one hand. She said something to George, then smiled when David crossed the small lobby to stop before her.

"Hi," she said.

"Hi yourself." He couldn't stop staring at her. Crossing his arms over his chest, he asked, "What are you doing here?"

"I took a chance you might be home and brought you these." She offered him the box.

A whiff of cinnamon hit him as he held it and he looked at her quizzically. "What's this?"

"Cinnamon buns from the Sweet Lovin' Bakery."

A weird warmth went through his chest. "That's very thoughtful of you. But what would you have done if I wasn't here?"

"Left them with the doorman. And texted you that they were waiting for you." Her teeth sank into her bottom lip and a lick of uncertainty flashed in her eyes. "I mean... you said you love them. So I got you some."

He wanted to devour her. "I do. And that's nice. But why?"

"Maybe I wanted to," she said. "And... maybe I wanted to see you again."

He nodded slowly. His whole body was aware of her, blood and warmth and want and need all mingling, lighting up every cell he had. "Would you like to come upstairs and share these with me? Maybe over a cup of coffee?"

"Yes," she said softly. Their eyes locked in a heated gaze. "I'd like that."

Chapter Six

"THIS IS DIFFERENT," Anna said, gesturing toward David's clothes as he puttered around in his small kitchen. "Jeans and a sweatshirt. I've only seen you in suits."

"I don't wear suits on the weekends," he said. He filled the French press with ground coffee as he added in a sassy, feminine tone, "To paraphrase Auntie Maxine, on the weekends, *I reclaim my time.*"

"Oh okay, Mizz Maxine Waters." Anna matched his knowing smile and leaned against the arch that vaguely split his tiny kitchen from the living room. "She's so badass."

"She certainly is."

"I wanna be her when I grow up."

"Me too."

"I met you on a Sunday, and you were wearing a suit."

"Unusual. I had to go to work and do face time on a conference call." He paused and turned to face her fully. "Wow, was that only a week ago today?"

"Does that make it, like, our anniversary or something?" she joked.

"Or something." He grinned and turned back to coffee

making.

In a few minutes, the rich smell of the dark roast coffee wafted through the air. Anna let her eyes run over his lean frame, lingering on how cute his ass looked in those jeans. He had a fantastic ass. "How tall are you?"

"Five-ten. Why?"

"Just curious. How old are you?"

"Thirty-five."

"When's your birthday?"

"April twenty-eighth." He shot her a bemused look over his shoulder before reaching for two stone-colored mugs. "Someone's full of questions."

"Just making small talk. This is a little awkward. I'm filling some spaces."

He turned to fully face her again. "Well, that's honest."

"I always am."

"Really?" He crossed his arms over his chest and fixed her with that intense stare of his. "Then I have a question. Why'd you leave before I woke up?"

Ah crap. She bit down on her lip. "That... well, that's a more complicated answer. We'll get to that later, maybe."

His eyes burned into her.

She almost squirmed under his gaze. "Ask me something else. Something easy, with a short answer, like the things I asked you."

He blinked, cleared his throat, and straightened. She wondered if he was pissed.

"Did you have a good time with me that night?" he asked bluntly.

"Yes," she said. She reached up to fidget with the edges of her hair. "I did."

He licked his lips and nodded. She could feel the air around them change. Suddenly it was crackling, like it was charged with something.

His arms dropped to his sides and he took a slow step toward her. "Would you maybe like to do that again some time?"

"Yes," she whispered.

"Is that why you're here tonight?"

"Just for that? No."

"Why else, then?" His eyes speared her, merciless.

Her heart rate sped up as she said, "Maybe I just like you a little."

"Yeah? If you did, you wouldn't have left without a goodbye."

"Maybe that's *exactly* why I did," she admitted quietly.

His jaw set as he stared at her. Stone-faced, he took another step toward her, closing the gap. They stood only a foot apart. "You didn't give me an inch when I came to see you the next night. If you like me, you hid that pretty well."

"It's a talent," she said, trying to sound flip.

He reached up to cradle her face in his hands, his thumbs caressing her cheeks as his hazel eyes held her captive. Her heart almost beat right out of her chest. She felt her face flush hot. God, he affected her.

"I'm glad you came by," David said softly. "Truth is, I haven't been able to stop thinking about you."

Anna felt her eyes widen. "Really?"

"Uh huh." His eyes swept over her face as his body edged even closer. "Can we drink the coffee later? I need to kiss you now."

"Okay," she whispered.

His mouth pressed to hers, soft and slow. The contact burned through her, a total infusion of heat. His hands held her face as he kissed her, taking what he wanted, sips and licks and nibbles. Her arms snaked around his waist, drawing him against her.

It was there. The magic she'd felt the other night. That first night, they'd kissed for hours, like teenagers, and it had been heavenly. He'd kissed her soft and sweet, he'd kissed her hot and hungry, consuming her, owning her, sending her into the stratosphere. His mouth was a goddamned wonder. And she hadn't imagined it; this thing between them was really there. His kisses were like a drug, and she wanted more.

His hands left her face to sift through her hair, then slide down her back to hold her closer, tighter. Their mouths tangled, demanding, taking, giving. She wanted him so much it shook her to the core.

"Can you stay a while?" he whispered against her lips.

"Yes," she whispered back.

"Can I take off some of your clothes, maybe?"

"Yes." She sank her teeth into his full bottom lip.

He let out a small groan and his fingers dug into her scalp. "You drive me a little crazy, Anna."

"Oh good." She grinned. "Let's see if I can drive you a *lot* crazy."

"Go for it," he growled, then took her mouth in a hot, consuming kiss. His mouth was demanding, almost punishing as he devoured her.

His hunger and urgency fueled hers. She pushed him back against the counter as they kissed, shoving her hands up under his sweatshirt, needing to feel his skin. Running her hands up his warm, smooth back, she gasped into his mouth as his teeth scraped hers, as his tongue worked magic against hers, as all the sensations washed over and battered her.

He pulled back enough to yank his sweatshirt up and over his head, dropping it to the floor. Smiling, her greedy hands slid up his chest, her fingertips sifting through the dark hair on his chest. "That's better," she said.

He grasped her waist and pulled her back to him, lowering his head to leave a hot, open-mouthed trail of kisses against her throat. Her breath caught as she raked her fingers up his back.

"This is insane," he whispered against her lips before kissing them. One of his hands fisted in her hair as the other grabbed her ass to hold her tighter against him.

She felt his erection against her belly and grinned. "It is.

And it's fun." He squeezed the globes of her arse as he bit her skin, making her gasp, "Ohhh… you're hot and you know it."

"You're hotter." He grabbed her hand and pulled her out of the kitchen. "This is okay, right?" he asked as he led her down the short hallway to his bedroom. "You're good?"

"Yes." She couldn't catch her breath, her heart raced, and her whole body felt like it was surging with energy and lust. But that wasn't even the best of it. The best of it was that he'd thought to check that she was okay with what they were doing, and were about to do. It was the look in his hazel eyes, the desire she saw burning there, mixed with a sliver of hope that she was indeed along for the ride and he wasn't assuming the wrong thing.

She loved how he wanted her. It was a heady rush, a boost to her ego and her long-underused libido.

She loved how he focused on her like she was all that mattered in the world. How his eyes drank her in as she pulled off her top to reveal her lacy purple bra, how his hands skated over her skin with a mixture of lust, reverence, and possession. How his mouth took hers like he owned her. Because in that moment, he did. And she loved every bit of it.

"Anna," he growled against her neck. "You're mine right now."

It was like he'd read her mind. It made her shiver in his arms. "I am."

"Want you too much…" He licked her skin, nibbled his way down.

"Take me, then," she breathed. "Take what you want. I want it too."

They kissed wildly, their hands frantic as they stripped each other's clothes away. He grabbed a condom from his nightstand and dropped it on the bed before lowering her to the mattress. They fell together ungracefully, both of them laughing. She couldn't remember the last time she'd laughed with a man in bed, especially one as intense and straitlaced as David. It was a delight.

Never breaking their kisses, he took her hand and put it where he wanted it. She liked his direct nature, and that it was more of a needy request than a command. The feel of his shaft, the hardness beneath the softness, the evidence of his desire for her, made her almost purr with satisfaction.

"I love how you feel," she whispered as she started stroking him.

His breath hitched before a long groan floated out of him. His arm slid beneath her to hold her closer and his head dipped so he could catch her nipple in his mouth, attacking it with a hungry, lustful vengeance. She sighed with pleasure, the sighs turning to moans when he captured it with his teeth. She ran her fingers through the short, thick waves of his hair and she arched her back to give him more of her. He growled and sucked, bit, licked her until she was writhing beneath him, then switched to her other breast to lavish equal attention there. His fingers dug into her hips as he drew her nipple even deeper into his hot mouth; she stroked him with long, firm strokes, feeling his hips starting to move in time to the pace she set.

His head lifted and he crushed his mouth to hers, kissing her until she was senseless. His hands moved over her with sureness and demand, caressing her skin as if he couldn't get enough.

When his fingers skimmed down her belly to explore between her legs, her breath stuttered and caught in her throat, releasing on a whoosh and a moan as he touched her. She stopped stroking his erection when his talented fingers ran lightly along her seam. As he teased her with featherlike touches she could barely breathe. The wetness there was almost embarrassing.

"God, that's so hot," he whispered against her mouth, his deep voice sending new shivers along her skin. "You're so there, Anna..."

"Take me," she begged in a raspy whisper. "Take it."

He plunged two fingers deep inside her, making her moan like an animal as her back arched off the bed. Her fingers clutched at the muscles in his shoulders.

"Like that?" he whispered against her ear, biting the lobe as he worked his fingers deeper.

"Yes," she gasped. "Oh God, yes." Her body moved in time with the rhythm his fingers set, her hips undulating on their own accord. "Christ, that's so good..." She reached for him and wrapped her hand around his shaft again. They panted and kissed and stroked, the fire building, the need sweeping them away.

"David," she panted. "I'm too close already. You're too good. Take me."

He kissed her hard, his hips grinding into her hand. "Put the condom on me, baby," he commanded in a strangled whisper.

She felt around on the mattress next to her, found it, ripped the foil open with her teeth. Rolling the condom down over his straining hard-on was sexier than she'd thought it'd be; it turned her on even more.

As soon as it was on, he shifted to roll on top of her and entered her with one smooth, powerful thrust. They both moaned at the incredible feel of joining. Her legs lifted to wrap around his hips as they moved together, the urgency building, their mingled breaths coming faster.

"Harder," she demanded breathlessly.

His hips slammed against hers, making her cry out. His hands tangled in her hair, pulling lightly as he took her harder, faster, his hips pummeling hers again and again as he drove deeper inside her. She felt the sensations circling through her, bringing her right to the edge.

Her orgasm hit fast, a wave of feeling searing through her, crashing over her. She cried out his name as she held on. Wave after wave of sensation made her delirious, mindless with pleasure. He grunted against her neck as he gave three more hard, fast thrusts, then he let go, his body stiffening, a long groan falling from his lips. She clung to him, milking out the moment as much as she could for both of them.

Their sweaty bodies stilled as they both fought to catch their breath, and he lifted his head to kiss her lips gently.

"Damn," he whispered, grinning as he pushed her tangled hair back from her face. "You good?"

"Oh my God, yes," she panted, meeting his eyes. "That was…"

He smiled, then dropped a long, lingering kiss on her lips. "Yeah. It was."

ANNA LAY ON her belly, her face turned to David in the dim light. Stretched out on his side, his free hand roamed leisurely over her body, his fingertips tracing the colorful designs etched into her velvety skin.

The flowered vine that crept along her arm. The tiny Celtic knot at the base of her neck. A shamrock on the inside of her wrist. A chain of flowers around her ankle. They all fascinated him. But what he liked most was the flurry of butterflies at the base of her spine. "These are really pretty," he said.

"Thanks." Her voice was thick and a little raspy, and her eyes were heavy, at half-mast. She looked and sounded sexy and dreamy and thoroughly sated. He loved it.

He counted the butterflies; there were five cobalt blue

ones, four hot pink ones, and two orange ones, all outlined in dark green. "Eleven. That's a lot. Must have hurt."

"Not much," she murmured. "And I had some whiskey to help me through."

He grinned. "People don't get tattoos unless they mean something. Every tat tells a story. So tell me a story. What do these butterflies mean?"

"Well, I know it's cliché, but first of all, I just love butterflies. But yes, these have a meaning. These butterflies represent my family," Anna said. "Lined in green for the Irish. The orange ones are my parents. Five boys, four girls. The Clan McKinnon."

David's brows furrowed. "Nine siblings? Thought you said you were one of eight. Am I remembering that wrong?"

"No. You remember right. Eight of us are living," she said, then cleared her throat. "The oldest, my brother Patrick, died when he was eighteen. Got stupid drunk one night and crashed his car into a wall. Died on impact."

"God, I'm so sorry," he murmured.

"Thank you. I barely remember him, honestly. I was a baby when he died. It hit Sean the worst. But I honor all of my family." She licked her lips. "I may have left them, and Ireland, but that doesn't mean I don't love them all. Like this, in a way, they're always with me." She shifted beside him and cleared her throat again. "I'm thirsty, mister. I need a drink."

"Stay here, I'll get it." David dropped a quick kiss on her

cheek and got out of bed. He padded down the short hall to the kitchen, thinking over things she'd said. For her to imprint all that ink on her skin, those butterflies... her family meant more to her than she let on. She was sentimental to do what she had.

He could relate. His family meant more to him than he let on, too. He'd been focused on his future since high school, and his family had always cheered his drive and supported him unequivocally. Every achievement he'd had, they'd beamed with pride. Every time he struggled, they'd been there for him. He and Jacob weren't close now, but they had been as kids. There hadn't been a falling-out; they were both just really busy in their high-powered careers. Their parents were loving and encouraging, making sure both Jacob and David had every opportunity possible to have the best in life—be it a toy, a car, their choice of college, travel...

That family clearly meant a lot to Anna only endeared her to him more.

The sun had disappeared while they'd been in bed, and the dark sky outside made David want to fall asleep, holding her close. He wondered if she'd let him.

As he sat on the edge of the bed, he handed her a bottle of water. She thanked him and sat up to drink. The comforter fell away, exposing her naked body, and a fresh surge of lust shot through him. His attraction to her was insane.

Then his stomach growled. They both laughed at the

sound.

"Do you have to go to work tonight?" he asked.

"No, I don't work on Sundays." She capped the bottle. "Sundays and Mondays are my weekend."

"Well, I have to go to work tomorrow," he said. "But—" He glanced at the clock on his nightstand. "It's past six. Why don't I order in some dinner? Or we could go out and get some?"

A slow smile spread across her face. "If we order in, we get to stay naked."

"Precisely why I suggested ordering in, Ms. McKinnon."

"I like the way you think."

"Dinner's on me, since you brought dessert."

"Seems fair. Thanks in advance."

"And... just one thing." He capped his water bottle and set it on the nightstand. "You never told me why you left last time." Her face bloomed with pink. He reached out and caressed her soft cheek. "We don't have to get into it. I won't push. But can you just promise me that from now on, you'll say goodbye when you leave?"

Her brilliant blue eyes widened. "From now on?"

"Yeah. We'll do this again." He stroked her jaw, her cheek, but his gaze never wavered. "We both want to, don't we?"

She bit down on her bottom lip, then said, "Yeah. I think we do."

"So then why not?"

"Sure. Why not?"

"But just do that one thing for me," he said softly, eyes on hers. "Don't slip out, don't leave without a word. Like we did something wrong. Or like you didn't really want to be here. Okay?"

"Okay," she whispered. She cleared her throat again. "Neither of those things are true, David. We didn't do something wrong, and if I didn't want to be here, I wouldn't be. Sorry I made you feel that way."

Something flowed through him, a mixture of relief and warmth. "Good. Now kiss me."

She leaned in to kiss him, her mouth warm against his.

Chapter Seven

Anna: *What r u doing?*

David: *Working. What are you doing?*

Anna: *I'm at work but the bar is dead tonight*

David: *Bummer.*

Anna: *You should come by. I have something for u*

David: *Oh yeah?*

Anna: *Yup. It's tiny, don't get too excited*

David: *Sometimes great things come in small packages.*

David: *No jokes, please.*

Anna: *LOL!*

David: *Didn't realize it was already after 7:00. I can come by soon.*

Anna: *Great. See u whenever*

WHEN DAVID WALKED into O'Reilly's an hour later, it was indeed quieter than he'd ever seen it. There were only five or six patrons, and none of them sat at the bar.

"Hiya, Suit!" Anna smiled brightly as he approached. She gestured around. "Told ya it was dead."

"How come?" he asked. He removed his overcoat and draped it over the empty barstool to his right. "Because it's a Tuesday?"

"Yeah. Tuesdays are the quietest nights. But this is morbid." She shrugged. "It happens."

As he loosened his tie and popped open his top shirt button, his eyes slid over her. Anna was in her regular work uniform: black top and leggings, her hair pulled back in a ponytail. Tiny orange and yellow maple leaf earrings dangled from her ears. On another woman, he'd probably have found them too kitschy, but on her, he found them adorable. He wanted to flip her onto the bar and kiss her senseless. "Fun earrings."

"Yeah, well, it's fall."

"It is. You look gorgeous, as usual."

"Thanks." She gave him an open once-over. "You fill out that suit nicely yourself." Tossing him a wink, she grabbed a cardboard coaster as he sat down. "Pick your poison."

"Um…" He leaned his elbows on the bar, scouring the wall behind her for ideas. "How about a hard cider tonight?"

"Interesting. Which kind?"

"Do you have Woodchuck?"

"Of course we do, babe."

As she filled a pint glass at the tap, he asked, "So what tiny thing did you have for me? Or are you drawing out the suspense?"

She grinned. "So impatient."

"Patience isn't one of my strong suits."

"I'll remember that. Give me a minute…" When the glass was full of golden liquid, she placed it before him. "Be right back. It's in my bag, back in the office."

David watched her go as he sipped the hard cider, savoring the crisp taste. Work had been chaotic as usual, and he was glad to be done with the day. He rolled his head on his shoulders, trying to loosen the knots there, then took a deep cleansing breath before stealing another sip. The other bartender, whom David had taken to calling Little John in his head because the guy was built like a mountain, took out a white rag and wiped down his end of the bar, making the polished mahogany gleam. A girl in the corner laughed loudly. Another deep breath, another sip, and David finally started to decompress from his busy day.

The song over the sound system changed to "Jingle Bell Rock" by Hall & Oates as Anna got back, ducking under and retaking her spot behind the bar. She held up a plastic CVS bag and said, "I had to get a few things today."

"So you got me what?" David joked. "Shampoo? Antacid tablets? You're too good to me."

"Always a smart-ass."

"You love that about me."

"I do, actually." Her eyes sparkled as she continued, "Anyway. When I saw these, I thought of you, so I got them." She dumped the contents of the bag onto the bar. There were several yellow-netted bags of chocolate coins wrapped in gold foil.

David had to laugh. "You got Hanukkah gelt for me?" He quickly counted; there were six little bags. "My first of the season."

"Really? Awesome!"

He took in her pleased smile and open excitement, and something warm flowed through his chest. "It's nice to be thought of. This was sweet of you. Thanks."

"Wait, there's something else…" She reached into the bag and pulled out a small, hot pink plastic dreidel. "Ta dah!"

He chuckled again. "Hot pink, huh?"

"I liked the color. I like bright colors."

He reached out to finger a lock of the fuchsia ends of her hair. "I know you do."

She smiled and spun the little dreidel. "Aha! I did it."

"It's not hard. It's like spinning a top."

"It is! But I've never done it before." When it stopped moving, she picked it up and did it again, then again. A delighted smile played on her lips as the dreidel spun in circles. "Doing it on the bar is the perfect place. Look at that. Smooth as can be."

"Yup." He smiled, charmed by her enchantment. "You're already a whiz."

"Not bad for an Irish girl, eh?"

"Not bad at all. I'm totally impressed."

She smiled wide and spun it again. "So, teach me, Suit."

"Teach you what?" he asked, confused. "We've already established you've mastered this skill."

"Noooo. How to play." She arched a thin brow at him. "There's a dreidel game, right?"

He was stunned for a second. "Um. Yeah. Yeah, there is." He took a long sip of cider as he watched her continuously spin the dreidel on the polished mahogany. "I haven't played it in a loooong time. I don't know if I remember the rules."

"Oh. Well..." Anna pulled her phone out of her back pocket. "I'll google it."

He gazed at her, mesmerized for a moment. "Okay."

"Open two of the bags," she instructed, not looking up as she scrolled on her phone. "I want to taste one of those."

He tore the netting on one of the bags and the gold coins dropped onto the bar. "They're just plain milk chocolate. Nothing special." He unwrapped one and held it out to her. "Here."

She thanked him and popped it into her mouth. "Oh. Yeah, okay. Regular chocolate."

"What'd you think it'd be?"

"I don't know. I've never had one before, so I wasn't sure what to expect. This tastes just like Nestlé or Hershey's, you're right."

As he opened another bag, making a small pile of the coins, he thought about how she'd done this for him. Something small but nice, and wanting to learn about his culture, one of his holiday traditions… and he wasn't sure what to make of that. It was sweet, thoughtful. He was touched by the gesture, he had to admit it.

"Okay!" She smiled broadly, put her phone down on the bar, and read, "It says that each player starts with about a dozen game pieces. That means the coins."

"Ya think?" he teased, winking at her.

"Smart-ass."

He opened another two bags of coins, making a pile, and counted out twelve for each of them. "What's next?"

"I have to tell you?"

"Yeah. I don't think I've played this since my age was in single digits."

"You haven't played with your nieces and nephews?"

"Nope. It's too old school for them. Nothing's plugged in." He gestured toward her phone. "Go on. Next."

She read briefly, then said, "We each put one coin in the center 'pot'. Then we take turns spinning the dreidel. Whichever side is facing up when it stops spinning, you take or give a coin from or to the pot." She frowned at him. "I don't know Hebrew letters. Can you at least show me that much? I mean, what kind of nice Jewish boy are you, anyway?"

He laughed heartily at her irreverence, then picked up the dreidel to show her the letters on each of the four sides. "This letter is *nun*. Nun means 'nothing'. So, you get that, you get nothing, and you do nothing. This one's *gimel*. You get that, you get everything in the pot. This one's *hei*, which means half."

"I get half the pot?"

"Like I've said, you're a fast learner. This last one is *shin*." He said in a singsong voice, "*Shin, shin, put one in.* That's the song to help you remember."

She smiled. "That was super cute."

He grinned back. "I can do cute."

"You really can."

He took two coins from each of their piles and put them between them, making a pot. "Okay. Now it's all coming back to me. You ready?"

"Sure."

She reached for the dreidel to spin it, but he grasped her hand. "Wait. What are the stakes?"

Anna huffed out a sardonic chuckle. "Spoken like a true finance shark."

"Well, what's the point of playing a game if there aren't any stakes?"

"Um, just for the fun of playing?"

"Nah. That's boring. C'mon, you're more competitive than that."

"Am I? I know *you* are."

He smirked wryly and conceded, "Guilty."

Her eyes lit up. "I have an idea. You want stakes? Let's play Truth or Dare dreidel, baby."

He laughed, hard. "What?"

"Well… since *nun* is nothing, now we'll make it something. You get *nun*, you get to ask a question. Nothing is out of bounds."

"Oh, sister, you are *on*." He unclasped her hand. "Ladies first. Go for it."

Anna shot him a saucy look, then picked up the dreidel and spun.

Four turns went between them before she got *nun*. "Okay!" She rubbed her hands together in wicked glee, making him chuckle. "We'll start with an easy one. How old were you when you lost your virginity?"

He rolled his eyes. "So cliché. That's your starter question?"

"Hey, I'm trying to take it easy on ya, Suit."

"Eighteen."

"Really?" Her brows lifted. "So late?"

"Late? What, I was supposed to be getting laid in junior high?"

She bit down on her bottom lip to try to hide her grin, but failed miserably.

"Whoa, wait," he countered. "How old were you?"

"Ummmm, this is *my* turn, Suit. You don't get to ask a question." She handed him the dreidel. "Your turn."

"Oh, okay. I see how this is." Grinning, he nodded at her with grudging admiration, then took his turn.

When he got *nun*, he immediately asked, "So how old were you?"

"Fifteen," she answered.

His eyes widened a drop. "Damn."

"Watch yourself," she warned.

"That's not derogatory," he said. "Just surprised. And some props. When I was fifteen, I was so clueless... I don't think I would've known how to."

Anna laughed hard. "Oh good Lord, that's precious."

The chocolate pile gained a few, lost a few. The song overhead changed to Bruce Springsteen's "Merry Christmas Baby".

"It's funny to play dreidel with Christmas music on," David remarked as he spun again.

"That's true." She smiled. "You're a good sport."

"And you're fun." The dreidel landed on *nun*. He paused, knowing what he really wanted to ask her. But would she answer?

"Go ahead," she said, leaning her chin on her hand. "Ask me anything."

He licked his lips and went for it. "Why'd you drop out of FIT?"

Her expression froze for a second, and he wondered if he'd crossed a line. She straightened up and her gaze dropped to the bar briefly before going back up to a spot over his shoulder. Then she said, "Because I realized I wasn't any good at design after all. The others there did rings around me. I knew I'd never make it. So I left."

David watched her face. She wouldn't look at him. She

looked at her fingernails, at the coins, at the wall. Past him, but not at him. "Hey. Anna," he said softly, reaching for her hand.

She let him take it and shrugged. "You have to know when to face reality and cut your losses. Sometimes you learn about things by failing at them."

"That's true," he said. "Actually, I think we learn more from our failures than from our successes."

She snorted and said, "You've probably never failed at anything."

"You are *so* wrong." He squeezed her fingers. "Would you look at me, please?"

She finally did, but her brilliant blue eyes were guarded. She looked vulnerable, a drop wary, and he hated that. "You think less of me because I don't have a college degree?" she asked, a hint of an edge to her tone. "Is that what this is about?"

He cringed inside and squeezed her hand tighter. "No. Not at all. I just wanted to know why you left, that's all. You said you came to America to go there, so I was curious why you'd leave."

"The truth is, I really came to New York because I was bored with my life back home," she said. "Sean sounded like he was having the time of his life. And I didn't know what I wanted to do with mine. I went through my first year at university, just taking liberal arts courses, but nothing spoke to me." She shrugged again. "Not everyone's like you, David.

Knowing what you wanted to do since you were a kid, and having the means to go after it." She slid her hand from his.

He leaned in, willing her to keep looking into his eyes. "I don't think less of you. I wish you believed me. More than that, I wish you didn't care."

"So do I." Her cheeks flamed with the admission.

"Annie!" Sean's voice boomed from the hallway that led to the office. "Can you c'mere a sec?"

"Saved," she breathed, and ducked under the bar to go back to the office.

His stomach still clenched, David reran their conversation in his mind. He'd hated that look in her eyes. She cared about his opinion of her. He cared that she cared. He cared that the look in her eyes was so uncomfortable, so vulnerable, that it made him want to pull her into his arms and soothe her. To assure her. To tell her he didn't give a crap about whether she'd gone to college or not, and he liked her just how she was.

He cared about her. What was supposed to be a casual thing... suddenly wasn't.

He knocked back the rest of the cider as he absorbed that.

Anna returned, ducking under to get behind the bar again. "Sean saw you were here. He said it's so dead here that I could leave if I wanted."

"Really? That's okay?"

"Yeah, why not? He'll still pay me, so it's all good. Just

no tips tonight, which I'm probably not gonna make anyway… might as well go home." She picked up the dreidel and gave it a spin. "Hey. Isn't this *gimel*?"

"Yup. You win the pot." He pushed the pile of chocolate coins to her. "There you go. Enjoy."

"I will, thank you." She opened one of the foil-wrapped coins and popped the piece of chocolate into her mouth. "Want one?"

"I want *you*," he said.

She locked eyes with him.

"Anna."

"Yeah?"

"Thanks for telling me about why you left. I admit, I've been curious. And clearly you didn't want to talk about it, but you did anyway."

"I don't wimp out," she said quietly.

"No, you don't," he said. "You're strong. You're a woman of substance and grit and fire. And man, that's hot."

She let out a tiny laugh as fresh pink bloomed on her pale cheeks.

"I'm trying to say I respect you, and I don't care that you didn't finish college," David said. "In my clumsy way."

Her gaze sharpened on his face, but she said nothing.

"If you feel bad about dropping out, I'm sorry to hear it," he said. "But I'm not judging you. Just saying."

She stared at him for a long beat, then nodded.

"Thank you for this." He gestured at the dreidel and the

gelt. "It was really thoughtful of you. I'm touched. I mean it."

Her eyes finally warmed. "I'm glad."

"And it was fun playing with you," he said.

Finally she smiled. "It was."

"So… would you come home with me?"

"Sure."

Chapter Eight

LATER THAT WEEK, late in the night, in that quiet, mystical zone where Saturday night turned into Sunday morning, David pulled Anna's head onto his chest and sifted his fingers through her hair. It always amazed him how silky it was. "So what are your plans for tomorrow? Anything good?"

"You bet," she said. "At three o'clock, Billy and I are doing our Christmas tree."

"Ah." David knew she and her friend, Billy Gonzalez, had shared an apartment for years, becoming roommates the year after she'd left FIT. That they'd met there the first day of her first year and clicked instantly. "Is this an annual tradition?"

"Yup. We do it before Thanksgiving, every year. Because I love Christmas. I know, I know, you think it's too soon."

"Yeah, it's too soon for *me*. But you do *you*. Anyone can do what they like."

"Oh good." She winked and snuggled closer into his side.

He exhaled a deep, cleansing breath as they held each

other. Then something occurred to him. "Wait, wait," he said. "What do you mean you're 'doing' your tree? I feel like I missed something. Don't you, like, go pick out a tree somewhere?"

"Yeah, if you're getting a live tree," she answered. "We have a fake one. So all we have to do is pull our boxed tree out of storage and set it up."

"A fake tree?" David made a face of faux outrage. "Aw man. That's a bummer."

"Why? Our building cranks the heat. A real tree would be dead within days. Trust me, we tried the first two years. We kept spraying it and everything, gave it extra water, but it was dried out in like two weeks. Both times, we had to get a second one. *That* was a bummer." She made a sad face. "So, we have a fake tree."

"I'm just so disappointed."

"I'm confident you'll get over it."

"But what about the smell of pine filling the room?"

"That's what scented candles are for, babe. Besides, I don't have to clean up pine needles for weeks afterward. Bonus."

David thought of how he'd seen people get Christmas trees in New York City: by buying them off the sidewalk. Random places that, for a few weeks, turned into small lots filled with firs, pines, and spruces. It had always struck him as odd, unnatural even, buying a Christmas tree off a busy city corner, surrounded by cement and skyscrapers. But at least they were real trees. Fake trees were so… fake. Then again, what did he know? Wasn't any of his business. "What other traditions do you and Billy have with the tree?"

Anna tipped her head back so she could look into his eyes as they talked. "We decorate it with Christmas music playing. And we drink hot cocoa spiked with peppermint schnapps. By the time the tree's fully decorated, we're pretty buzzed. Then we order in a pizza and watch a Christmas movie. We have a few mutual favorites, so we rotate the choices."

"Sounds like fun," David said with a smile.

"It is." She tenderly stroked his stubbled cheek, feathering with her fingertips. Leaning in, she trailed some kisses along his jawline.

Enchanted by her small show of affection, he gazed into her deep blue eyes. "Um… hope I'm not overstepping, but any chance I could tag along tomorrow?"

Her eyes widened. "Really? Would you like to?"

"Yeah, it sounds fun. I've never decorated a Christmas tree before. And I'd like to reciprocate on the holiday front, since you were so sweet the other day about getting me a dreidel and gelt." He trailed his fingers along the side of her face. "And who doesn't like spiked hot chocolate?"

Anna smiled wide and bright. "I'd love it if you came over to hang with us. I'd love to watch you decorate a Christmas tree for the first time. That's special." She moved in to drop a kiss on his lips, pure sweetness. "Yes, please join us."

ANNA'S STOMACH WAS a bit wobbly with nerves. David had never been to her apartment before. He lived in a luxury building; she lived in an old building. There wasn't an elevator, and it was a walk up of three flights to her floor. She'd always thought her building, though ancient, had a lot of charm and the bohemian flavor that the East Village used to be known for before gentrification. Now, through David's eyes, she wondered if all he would see was a former tenement building, age, and a bit of decay. Her building was as clean as an older one could be, but it wasn't upscale or fancy, not like his.

She was mad at herself for even worrying about what he'd think. She liked her building. It suited her needs just fine. She wasn't embarrassed or anything; she just knew it would show him plainly another example of how different their worlds were. When they were alone, talking in the bar or together in bed, the differences seemed to disappear. But this... was another step into each other's worlds, and in a way, putting them out in the light. Introducing him to one of her closest friends, having him over, letting him in on one of their most cherished Christmas traditions... She couldn't help it—she was a bit nervous.

But David was in a great mood when he arrived at their apartment. Anna watched as his eyes canvassed the space, silently but thoroughly assessing, and would've given anything in the world to know what he was thinking.

"Brought these," David said, holding up the box.

"Sweet Lovin' Bakery?" she asked.

"You bet. Hope you guys like the best Christmas cookies in the Village."

"Maybe the *West* Village, honey," Billy said, getting up from the couch with a smile. "Them's fightin' words. I'll have to sample one or eight to really make sure."

David laughed and shook Billy's hand as he introduced himself.

Anna watched them chat, bemused. The men were very different, but seemed to warm to each other pretty quickly. David looked adorable in his navy fleece hoodie, dark gray Henley, and jeans. And he seemed relaxed, not quite as intense as usual. She realized his whole demeanor changed when he wasn't wearing a suit. He was quicker to smile, not wound up as tight. As if being out of his work outfit gave him the freedom to not have to cultivate his work persona, allowing him to be his truest self. She wondered if he even knew that about himself.

As if reading her thoughts, he went to her and gave her a quick kiss. "You're staring at me."

"Yeah, well, I like looking at you."

"Oh yeah?"

"Mm hmmmm."

His hazel eyes lit up. "And here I was thinking how

damn cute you look."

She struck a pose in her tight red velvet top and green leggings with candy canes on them. "I pulled out my stash of Christmas clothes! I'm so happy."

He chuckled. "Your being happy makes me happy. And this looks great too." His hands skimmed down her sides, over her ribs. "This velvet is soft. I like it."

"Okay, okay, you're both so adorable, I can't stand it," Billy said. He shoved another cookie into his mouth as he pulled the pieces of tree out of the box. "Now come help me with these branches, gorgeous."

Anna nudged David's side. "He's talking to you, not me."

"Of course he was," David said, and sat beside Billy on the couch.

"Here." Billy handed him a few metal branches. "Start with these."

Anna breathed a sigh of relief. She and Billy had been friends for a long time. His inner barometer for picking good men had always been dead-on—even more so for her than for himself. Anyone she'd ever brought around that Billy didn't like... they were the ones who'd ended up burning her. He'd been right almost every time.

So if Billy seemed to like David, was already comfortable with him, that was a very good sign indeed.

Anna bit her lip to keep from laughing as she watched David. He was clearly confused, the poor thing. His brows furrowed as he examined the base of the tree stand, then the holes to put the branches into… The utter consternation on his handsome face amused her to no end. She grabbed her phone from the end table and snapped some pictures.

"You look lost, sweetie," Billy said.

"I'm just figuring out how this thing works," David replied.

"Some brilliant investment banker you are," Billy joked. "It's not rocket science."

David shot him a look, but was clearly in on the joke.

"Ivy League and you can't figure this out?" Anna teased.

"Well," David cracked, "they didn't teach Putting Fake Christmas Trees Together 101 at Cornell. Definitely not in Hebrew school."

Anna and Billy dissolved into giggles.

"I'm going to start the kettle," Anna said. "Spiked hot cocoa coming up!" Before she went, she started the Bluetooth speaker. Her Christmas mix kicked off with The Waitresses's "Christmas Wrapping" and she turned up the volume with a smile before slipping into the kitchen.

As she set the filled kettle on the stove to boil, Anna thought about her situation with David. Situation, because she wasn't sure what to call it, or them. Whatever it was they were doing, they were doing it a lot. In only a few weeks, Anna had ended up at David's apartment three or four nights a week. It had escalated quickly. She still was wary of the whole thing. But they couldn't get enough of each other.

And here he was, in her apartment now for the first time, bantering with Billy and helping them decorate for Christmas. It was both a thrill and made her nervous. She usually liked going back to his place for two reasons. One: he had his own place, so she and David had privacy to have the wild sex they kept enjoying. Two: she liked that she could leave. In that way, she kept the parameters on her terms. Felt like she had some control.

She needed that. Because David was a quietly strong, quietly powerful man, and something in her responded to that more than she'd thought it would. She liked that. She liked *him*. They had some kind of yin and yang thing going on, and it worked.

Sometimes she wasn't sure what drew them together besides the undeniable chemistry. They were so different. She was open, vocal, always chasing the laughs and the light. He was sober, simmering with intensity, wired with some kind of laser focus and energy he brought to everything he did... especially sex with her. He was incredible in bed, or they were incredible together, she didn't know. She didn't know what she was doing with him. But she didn't want to stop.

She peeked into the living room to see what they were up to. They were halfway done getting the tree together, a good start. Billy said something she couldn't hear over the music, and David laughed. His laugh always filled her with something golden, like spotting a unicorn or like she'd caught a glimpse of sunshine in a cloudy sky. Sensing he was being watched, he glanced up at her and winked. She grinned at him and ducked back into the kitchen.

She couldn't wipe the grin off her face. He was good to her. He was respectful and attentive, with a dry wit that made her laugh and a sweet smile that made her go gooey inside. Every time he walked into the bar, her stomach gave a wobbly flip and her blood started humming in her veins. So every time, when he'd lean in and murmur in her ear, "Come home with me?" she went willingly. And the days had turned into weeks, and she... was smitten. Damn. She really was.

In the mornings, after their long and lusty nights, David always woke for work at seven-thirty. So if she opted to sleep over, he'd wake her too. He always kissed her awake and offered her coffee; she always declined and pulled away, getting out of bed to put her clothes on. He had to get ready for a long day, and she didn't want to distract him any further, knowing as it was he'd be operating on only a few hours' sleep. Before he could even hop in the shower, she'd kiss him goodbye and leave. Sometimes he tried to get her to stay for a little morning action, but most times, she'd gently but unmistakably insist on leaving.

It felt safer that way.

She wanted to trust it, whatever this growing thing between them was. But she just couldn't let her guard down completely. She'd been swept away before, and how had that worked out?

So she kept telling herself it wasn't a relationship. It just needed to be enjoyed while it lasted. Before he changed his mind about sleeping with a bartender and went back to his dignified wealthy world. He was a man used to getting what he wanted, of that she was sure. She didn't want to bend to him too easily. Or maybe at all. Because she'd been with a man like him before, and the price had been too high.

As long as things stayed light, she'd be fine. Now, if she could just tell her heart to stay with that plan, things would be great.

"Anna!" Billy called. "We're done, the tree looks like a tree! Time to decorate this thing! Where's my cocoa?"

"Hold on..." Anna grabbed the bottle of peppermint schnapps and poured a generous amount into each steaming mug. Balancing all three in her hands, she carefully made her way out to the living room.

David rushed to help, grabbing two of the mugs from her. "Nice balancing act."

"Occupational perk." She watched him hand Billy a mug as the song changed to Lena Horne's swinging version of "Jingle Bells". The tree stood in the corner she and Billy always set it in. "Hey, look at that! It's a Christmas tree! It's naked, but it's a tree!"

"I feel very accomplished," David said.

"You should!" Billy said. "You did a great job for your first time, sweetie." He patted David on the back with his free hand. "Now we're really gonna break you in: untangling the lights."

David didn't miss a beat. "Bring it on."

Anna smiled brightly and raised her mug in a toast. "Merry Christmas and Happy Hanukkah, boys."

"Feliz Navidad!" Billy cried with gusto.

"L'chaim!" David said, and tapped his mug to each of theirs. "That's Hebrew," he stage whispered to Billy. "It means, 'To life'."

"I know, Banker Boy," Billy said. "You think you're the first Jewish boy I've met in this town? Suckah, please."

"Just making sure," David said. "I'm nothing if not thorough." He winked at Anna before sipping his cocoa. His eyes flew wide as he exclaimed, "Mmm! This is great! Where's this been all my life?"

She laughed and gazed affectionately at him. He was adorable and witty and gorgeous and she wanted to throw herself into his arms. Lord help her, she was head over heels.

Chapter Nine

ANOTHER NIGHT AND here I am, David thought as he entered O'Reilly's. The weeks were flying by. It was just past eight, and he'd asked Mike to meet him there for a few drinks. Getting to watch Anna from across the room and hanging out with his friend would be a fun way to pass the time until she got off work.

But when he walked further inside, he didn't see Anna behind the bar. There were three men, instead of two men and Anna, the usual Saturday lineup. He frowned. He'd texted Anna around four o'clock, and she'd said she was working until one A.M. He went up to the bar. The closest bartender had his back turned to him as he reached for a glass.

"Excuse me," David said. "Sorry to bother you, but isn't Anna working tonight?"

The man turned and David braced himself. It was Sean, her brother. They had the same bright blue eyes. But Sean's hair was a darker shade of blond, and his beard matched it. "Aye," Sean said, "she's here. Just in the back, taking her dinner break."

David nodded. "You're Sean, right?"

"I'm sure you know I am. You're here often enough." Sean held out a hand. "We haven't been formally introduced, David."

"Good to finally meet you." David shook his hand and added, "You have a great place here. I like it."

"Thanks." Sean assessed him for a long beat. "I also have a great sister. Don't fuck her over. Okay?"

David couldn't help but grin. "I agree, you have a great sister. We enjoy hanging out. I have no intention of fucking her over. But I'm sure she'd appreciate your protectiveness."

"I'm sure she wouldn't. But I don't care." Sean shrugged, not breaking eye contact. "Big brother rights."

David nodded as he considered that. "Is this where you tell me if I break her heart, you'll break my legs?"

Sean barked out a laugh. "Something like that." He rubbed his beard and blew out a breath. "Ya want a drink?"

"Sure. Julius would be good."

"Coming up." Sean moved away to get the IPA.

David watched him. Sean was a few inches taller than him and had the wiry frame of a lightweight boxer. He had to give the guy props for looking out for his sister, even if there was a trace of genuine menace in the Irishman's eyes. David was strong enough, but had never been in a fistfight in his life. He had no doubt that Sean could likely kick his ass. He hoped to never find out.

"So," Sean said as he set the glass down. "She's told me

very little about you. Just that you live in my neighborhood, you're Jewish, you work a lot, and you're an investment banker."

"That pretty much covers the basics," David said amiably, and took a sip of his drink. "Anything else you want to know?"

"Nope." Sean shrugged. "Anna seems fine, so that's all I need to know for now."

"I'm, uh… glad she seems fine." David wasn't sure what to say, and he took another sip of his beer.

Sean just stared at him.

"I think she's great," David said earnestly. "Really."

Just as Sean nodded, Anna appeared, walking behind the bar and up to them. She looked from one man to the other, curiosity all over her face. "Well, what do we have here? Some friendly girl talk?"

"I introduced myself to your friend here," Sean said, "since you haven't seen fit to yet."

"Aha. Well. Sorry I missed the fun." She tossed David a sunny smile. "Hiya, handsome. Nice to see you."

"Nice to see you too." He smiled at her before taking another sip.

Anna looked up at her brother. "Thanks for covering for me. I'm back. You can go do whatever boss things you do back in the office."

"You dismissin' me, Annie?" Sean asked, only half teasing.

"I sure am. Three's a crowd. See ya." She gave him a smack of a kiss on his cheek, then a gentle shove. "Go on. Get lost."

"You're in *my* bar, miss," Sean growled, but started to move away. "Good meeting you," he said over his shoulder.

"Good to meet you too," David said. Once Sean was out of earshot, he said, "Well, that was interesting."

"Was it now?" Anna leaned across the bar and stole a quick kiss before showering him with a smile made of mischief and sunshine. "What'd I miss? Tell me!"

"He just... introduced himself to me. He knew who I was. And he threatened to break my legs if I don't treat you right."

"He did not," she said on a laugh.

"No, he didn't. Not exactly. The threat was more implied than stated."

"Good Lord." Anna rolled her eyes. "Well, he's a little overprotective. Sometimes I think he still thinks I'm a kid."

"He clearly means well. He obviously cares about you. No issue with that." David smiled at her. "Hey. You look gorgeous. As always."

She rolled her eyes again, but couldn't hide the sparkle of pleasure in them. "Thanks."

He reached out to hold her hand, interlacing their fingers, just wanting the contact. "Think he'd really beat me up?"

"Only if you do me wrong. So don't."

"I won't."

"Good. He was a bit of a brawler back in his teens. I wouldn't mess with him."

"So I shouldn't tell him how I plan to take you home later and have my merry way with you?" David grinned wickedly. "Throw you down on the couch because I can't even wait to get you to the bed, practically tear your clothes off, take you hard, and make you scream with lust and passion?"

Her cheeks turned rosy, but her eyes widened. She loved the sound of that, and he loved that she did. "That might gross him out," Anna said, grinning back. "So nah."

"Okay then."

"You can tell *me* more about that, though. That sounds hot."

"It does, right?"

"STAY OVER TONIGHT," David said. They'd just had their second round of sexy times, and he could still hear the echoes of her moans in his ears. He'd taken her on the couch first, as he'd told her he would at the beginning of the night, then led her to his bed for a slower, more leisurely romp. Now he trailed his fingers up and down the smooth skin of her back, down over the curves of her ass and back again. "Tomorrow's Sunday. The one day neither of us work."

"I know," she said. "You're not telling me something I

don't know."

He gave her ass a pinch and she yelped.

"So stay. When you stay, it's nice. Like how we went out to brunch last weekend before I went to your apartment... I had a great day with you." His fingertips made tiny circles around the butterflies at the base of her spine. "You had a good time too, right?"

"Yes. It *was* nice," she agreed, almost like she was admitting something she didn't want to admit.

"Okay. So let's do it again."

She didn't answer.

His brows drew together as he studied her. "You have plans tomorrow?"

"Actually, no," she said. "I don't."

"So..." Nah, screw that. David let his voice trail off. He wasn't going to beg her to stay. He just was curious why she was ambivalent.

She licked her lips, cleared her throat. She pulled away to sit up and reached for the glass of water he'd left for her on his nightstand. "Okay. I'll stay." She sipped.

"Okay, great." He watched her, sensing something, wondering about her hesitation in accepting his invite. Her pale skin had red patches where his stubble had scraped her, her lips were swollen from his kisses, and her hair was a little tangled. Male pride mixed with infatuation, stirring his blood. He'd made her look like that. Like a woman who'd been thoroughly ravaged and had thoroughly enjoyed herself.

"You're beautiful," he murmured.

"I am not," she scoffed. She blushed and looked away as she sipped more water.

"Yeah, you are." He looked at her like she was insane. "I think you are, Anna."

"Well, thank you." She set the glass aside and lay back down beside him.

He pulled her close so he could kiss her. He loved kissing her; he could kiss her for hours. And Anna seemed to like the long kissing stretches too. David hadn't enjoyed kissing a woman like this since college. He and his girlfriend, Wendy, had lain on his bed with music playing and made out for hours. He'd loved her, so he loved making out with her, just holding her and kissing her...

He wasn't in love with Anna, but damned if it wasn't similar to those times. The pure euphoric sensation was very, very similar. Anna was a phenomenal kisser, so really, that was the biggest part of it. But he also really liked her, so he liked kissing her. Like it'd been back then...

But unlike back then, when he'd been a lovesick puppy for Wendy, he hadn't told Anna how much he liked her. Part of him felt like he didn't need to; the fact that he kept coming back for more and more was probably a pretty good tip-off. But there were also moments like this one, where something in her body language, something in her eyes, told him instinctively that she wouldn't want to hear it. She liked keeping him at an arm's distance. He'd figured that out. He wasn't sure why, but he wanted to keep seeing her, so he kept his slowly growing feelings to himself. He wasn't a fool; you didn't fix something that wasn't broken. You left it as it was.

Anna nestled into his side, resting her head on his shoulder as her fingers played in his chest hair. "Thanksgiving's on Thursday," she said into his skin.

"I know. Can't believe it's here already."

"Me neither. So what are your plans for it?"

"Going home," he said. "To my parents' house. Whole family will be there."

"That sounds nice. Are you going for the whole weekend?"

"Nah. I'll go out on Thursday morning, get there early." His fingertips skimmed along her back, up and down along the velvet. He could never seem to stop touching her when she was near him. "I'll probably come back to the city some time on Saturday, late afternoon." He shifted so he could look into her eyes as they talked. "What about you? Hope you don't have to work?"

"Well, yeah, I am. Wednesday night, the night before Thanksgiving, is a huge bar night. I'll make great money." She tore her gaze from his, seemingly intent on the patterns her fingers made along his chest. "On Thanksgiving, the bar won't open 'til five. But I'm not working on Thanksgiving. I'm going with Sean and Cassandra out to Long Island. Her parents live there, and they have a big family holiday, so they always bring me along. I'll stay over with them, and come back to the city on Friday and work that night."

"Yeah, I guess Thanksgiving weekend must be busy, with all the tourists and holiday shoppers and all that crap," David said. "I didn't think of it that way because you don't work retail, but it's the same thing in that you work with people..."

"You betcha. So yes, I'm working every night this week as usual, except for Thursday." Anna slipped her foot in between his, curling into his side with a yawn.

"Can I see you on Saturday night, then?" he asked. "When I get back? I could come to the bar around nine or ten, if that's okay. And you could sleep over that night, and we could hang out on Sunday."

"Again? Sounds like a pattern." Her tone was light, joking, but she wouldn't meet his eyes. "You makin' plans with me, mister?"

"I'm trying to."

He willed her to look at him. She still wouldn't.

It hit him like a bolt from above. This wild, open, fun, brazen woman... was unnerved. Talking like this, making plans, made her nervous. Something about that implied more, and that made her nervous. Well goddamn.

He tipped up her chin with a firm grasp, gently forcing her to look into his eyes. "Is that all right with you, me trying to make plans that far ahead? Or you'd rather not? Just tell me. I can take it."

"No, it's fine." Her cheeks bloomed with color. "It's all right with me."

"What's going on, Anna?" he asked softly. Still holding her chin, he stroked her skin with the pad of his thumb. "What's up?"

Her rosy face deepened, turning almost the same magenta as the streaks in her hair. "I just…" She wiggled out of his embrace and sat up, pulling the blanket up to cover her chest. "What are we doing, David? I mean… what is this? Us? This thing?" She gestured between them. "What is this?"

He leaned up on one elbow to look at her. "I don't know. But I like it, whatever this is."

She smiled softly, but her blue eyes pinned him.

"You surprise me, Anna." He sat up too. "You didn't strike me as the type who needed, or even liked, labels."

Her eyes narrowed. "We've been sleeping together for almost a month now. You keep asking me to stay over. You want to make plans on a holiday weekend. Yeah, I'm curious what's in your head. So I asked. Sorry, I won't again."

She moved to get out of bed and he shot out his hand to grasp her forearm. "Hey. Stop." He lifted his other hand to hold her shoulder. "Let's talk."

Her body stiffened beneath his gentle grip. "We are talking."

"No. You asked me a pointed question, and I'm going to answer it." He leaned in to kiss her lips. "That wasn't a sneer, what I said about you wanting to label this. You're such a free spirit; it just surprised me that you asked for a qualifier about us. That's all."

"A qualifier, eh?"

"For lack of a better word right now, yes."

"Uh huh." A saucy grin spread across her face.

"So. Us. This thing. We're…" He moved both hands down to intertwine his fingers with hers. They sat facing each other, their hands locked. "We clearly enjoy each other, both in and out of bed. But especially *in* bed."

"True on both counts," she agreed, her grin widening.

"You're a lot of wonderful things in one package. I mean… yes, I like your seemingly insatiable sexual desires, dirty mouth, incredible body, and mattress skills." He looked into her eyes to make sure she knew he was teasing, but his voice dropped as he admitted, "I also like you for the more important things. Your sass, your light, your being pragmatic though you have a whimsical nature, your soft heart that you try to hide, the smart, solid head on your shoulders. Everything combined? Of course I keep coming back for more."

He watched her face as she took in his confession. It was fascinating, the lightning-fast display of emotions that whirred through her blue gaze. Delight, surprise, wariness… and something possibly like hope.

"Maybe you like me too?" he murmured, squeezing her fingers in his.

She was so still. Was she breathing?

"Maybe you like me even if it's just for the equal mattress

skills?" he joked, hoping to break through her silence.

Finally, she gave a little nod. "Yeah," she whispered. "Maybe even for more than just that."

He peered harder into her eyes. "That was hard for you to admit, wasn't it."

She nodded again, swallowing before she said, "Guys like you... have chewed me up and spat me out."

His stomach churned at that. In the back of his mind, he'd suspected as much, but hearing the actual confirmation made him sigh. "I thought you didn't like guys like me, so you wouldn't have dated guys like me."

"I did once. It was... a mistake." She shrugged and tried to pull her hands from his. He held on. She was always trying to run from him, to slip away, to avoid things.

And he said that to her.

Her eyes went wide.

"So tell me why," he said gently. "I want to know. Was it that guy who you bumped into the day we met? The one who was married?"

Her eyes widened. "Good memory."

"It wasn't that long ago, sugarpop."

"He was part of it, but actually, worse stuff happened before him."

David absorbed that and asked quietly, "What happened?"

She shook her head. "Doesn't matter."

"Yeah, it does. It's affecting how you interact with me.

So clue me in."

"I don't want to talk about it, David."

He stared at her. Her voice was stern and low. She meant it.

But he didn't want to push her into a stonier place. He had a feeling her stubborn streak was as formidable as his. So with a sigh and a nod, he said, "Okay. I won't push. For now. But maybe eventually you'll trust me enough to tell me about whatever happened."

She stared back and only said, "Maybe."

"In the meantime…" He lifted her hands to his lips, kissing the backs of them. "What are we, what is this? That's what you asked. Well, we're seeing each other. A lot of each other. So… I guess you could say we're kind of dating."

"Even though we don't go out on dates?"

"What?"

"We don't exactly go *out*," she said. "You come and meet me at the bar, then we come back here to have marathon sex. *Sometimes* we go out, like when I hang out with you on Sundays. But mostly, we're in bed. So I'm not sure if we're actually dating."

"Well, when you put it like that…" He quirked a silly grin. "It actually sounds better than dating, gotta say. No?"

She laughed. "I guess so."

He caressed her hands, her forearms. "Well, do you want to get out of bed more often and go do more things?"

She shrugged. "Don't get me wrong, this works for me.

But... yeah, it might be nice. If we're saying we're dating. I guess."

He stared at her harder. This was the most vulnerable and uncomfortable he'd ever seen her. It was a game-changer. It made him feel strangely protective of her.

And he went for it anyway. "So... next scary question. Do you want to start dating exclusively? Because if that's on the table, I'd like to say that I would."

"Really."

"Yes. I like you, I like what we have going on, and I'm not looking to meet anyone else. So... yeah. Yes."

She bit down on her bottom lip. "Um..."

His stomach gave a little flip. Her hesitation threw him for a loop. "Look, you don't have to give me an answer right now, Anna. Think about it. It's fine." He gave her hands another squeeze. "I'm not going anywhere."

She stilled at that. "You're not?"

"No. Not anytime soon. I told you why." He pulled her in, wrapped his arms around her, and kissed her deeply. Kissing her always made sense. So he'd stick to that for now, a great way to make himself chill out while she pondered what he'd offered.

She kissed him back fervently, warming to him in a heartbeat. She usually did.

But his brain wouldn't stop. He didn't like that she hadn't given him an automatic "yes". His ego didn't like it. And he didn't like feeling vulnerable or off his game. But that was part of this whole thing with Anna: he *was* a bit off his game, doing things he didn't usually do, feeling things he hadn't expected to feel, and just rolling with it. Breaking out of his box with her felt too good to stop.

This whole thing had been crazy from the start, and he was finding he liked the crazy. For someone who was used to being in control of his surroundings, he was letting her take the lead, following her lead, and really had been from the start. She clearly had her secrets and wasn't willing to share them. For now, he was fine with that. For now.

Chapter Ten

DAVID REACHED FOR her hand and Anna let him tug her closer as they walked. It was a crisp, cool day, a perfect November afternoon. It had taken them most of the day to finally get out of bed, but they were finally out and about.

"Where are we going, anyway?" she asked him.

He quirked a grin and said, "Not really sure."

"Huh. You're always so focused. You like to plan. I didn't think a man like you would be happy just walking around for the sake of walking around."

He glanced down at her. "Hmm. Well… you're not wrong, actually." A little self-deprecating laugh slipped out of him, and she adored him for it. "Maybe that's why we should do this. Just… roam. End up wherever we end up."

"Look at you, up for an adventure," she teased.

"Lady, *you* are an adventure." He kissed her forehead as they walked. "And I'm loving the ride."

Her insides wobbled at his words. She stole a long look at him. He got a little more handsome every time she saw him, if that was possible. He hadn't shaved, and dark stubble coated his strong jaw, accentuating his full lips that she adored. He'd pulled on jeans, runners, a navy sweater under his dark brown barn coat. Ray-Bans hid his eyes but they made him look sexy as hell. He looked like he'd stepped off the pages of a J.Crew catalog. And it shocked her how much she enjoyed that. Her straitlaced yuppie banker.

"Is there anywhere in particular you want to go?" he asked. "Name it and we'll go. I'm game."

She shrugged. "Nah. I'm glad to just be out with you."

"Oh yeah?"

"Yeah."

He released her hand and slid his arm around her shoulders, holding her closer as they strolled up Sixth Avenue. "Sounds good to me."

The sun shone down on them, the wind blew her hair back, people walked all around them. She nestled into David's side and let her heart take in the warmth.

"I REMEMBER YOU," Billy said to his roommate as she entered their apartment.

"Hi, love," Anna said, closing the door behind her. She dropped her keys into her bag and her bag onto the soft chair in the corner. A glance at the clock told her it was close to eleven. She'd been with David for the entire day. And it still had made her a little sad to say goodbye to him. Amazing, that. She yawned as she sat on the couch beside her friend.

"How've ya been, Billy Boy?"

"Fabulous as always," he answered. "Did three loads of laundry, ate my weight in pineapple pizza, and wasted too much time on Grindr."

"I dunno," she joked, "sounds productive to me."

"Another earthshaking Sunday." Billy rolled his eyes. "You spent the day with Banker Boy, I assume?"

"Yup."

"Have fun?"

"Yup."

"Good for you." Billy's dark eyes narrowed. "That boy toy is becoming a habit."

"He is," she admitted. "And a hard one to break."

"Who said you have to break it? He's clearly crazy about you."

"You think so?"

"I think so." Billy aimed the remote at the flat screen to mute and pause the cooking show he'd been watching. He pushed her hair aside to examine her stubble-scraped neck. "And hey, you look good and used to me. I'd say shut up and enjoy it."

Anna snorted out a laugh. "*You* shut up."

"Never."

"I'd expect nothing less." She shot him a grin, then yawned again. "I'm wiped. I'm going to take a shower, then go to bed."

"Exhausted from a sex marathon with a hot banker. I'm

so jealous." Billy gave a dramatic sigh and winked at her. "Sweet dreams, hon."

"Good night, you." Anna dropped a kiss on his forehead before shuffling off to the bathroom.

As she took a quick shower, she recalled the feel of David's body against hers, his hands, his mouth, his hardness deep inside her. If it was possible to be physically addicted to someone, she was to him. Usually, after the first few exciting weeks of a fling, the excitement wore off, the lust lessened somewhat, and she got bored. That wasn't happening with David. In fact, the opposite was happening. She just wanted him more and more.

Not just his body. All of him.

What a lovely day they'd had together. Hanging out in bed until after one, going out for a long walk, sipping coffee in a café, stealing kisses from each other wherever they went, and bantering all the while. For people from opposite worlds, the whole "opposites attract" thing seemed to be working for them so far.

But the night before, when he'd brought up dating, she'd frozen like a deer in the headlights. She'd clammed up and swallowed the words she'd really wanted to say. *I like you too. I want you too. I love that you want to date only me. I'm surprised and flattered and I want that too. I'm into this as much as you seem to be, and I'm going to take a chance and believe you mean it. Yes, let's give this a try, why not? Take me, I'm yours.*

But she hadn't said any of that. Anna Gail McKinnon, usually bold and brave in word and deed, unrestrained, risk taker, badass... was a goddamned scaredy-cat. That was the truth of it here. And that shamed her.

She dried off, wrapped the towel around herself, then used the smaller towel to wrap her wet hair turban-style. Staring at herself in the mirror, she said to her reflection, "You stupid wimp."

She brushed her teeth, ran a comb through her damp hair, then went to her room, knowing who she needed to talk to. Problem was, since Ireland was five hours ahead, that made it four-forty in the morning in Dublin. So she sat on her bed to send her friend Toni a few long, pathetic texts. Toni was one of her best friends in the world. She also was one of her sisters-in-law now, since she'd married Anna's brother Gavin three years ago.

When Toni and Gavin had met and fallen hard and fast for each other, Anna had been the one to encourage Toni to get out of her own way and let herself enjoy Gavin. The irony of the parallel situation now wasn't lost on her, and she was sure it wouldn't be lost on Toni either.

After texting, Anna got into bed and fell quickly into a hard sleep.

When she opened her eyes and glanced at her clock, it was past eleven in the morning. She'd had a long, awesome sleep and was grateful for it. Stretching in her bed, she yawned and reached for her cell phone from the nightstand.

Several texts waited for her.

> **David:** *Good morning. I'm at work and you're probably still sleeping. Doesn't seem fair. Hope you slept well. Talk to you later.*

> **Toni:** *OHHHHH GIRL. This is too much to do over texts. Call me. We'll play phone tag until we talk. Hang in there, love u!*

> **Vince Hansen:** *Hey Anna, how r u? Have a gig for u if u want it. Fancy corporate holiday party in midtown on 12/11. Call me if interested*

> **Cassandra:** *Hi lady. Be here at 9 am on Thurs. Uber is taking us out to LI & will be here then. I know that's early for you, but if you want a ride… ☺*

Anna needed coffee.

But first she answered David's text.

> **Anna:** *It's 11:17 & I just woke up. So ur right. I know how much u love to be right, so just thought I'd make ur day. Ttyl*

She grinned as she hit send. David didn't like text speak; like Cassandra, he preferred writing words out, grammar snobs that they were. As with Cass, Anna knew her texts likely made him twitch a little, and that was part of the fun.

"Coffee," she moaned aloud, and got out of bed.

After downing two cups of coffee and eating half a buttered bagel, she went back to her room and tried to call Toni.

"Hey!" came Toni's voice. "You got me on the first try! Lucky us!"

Anna smiled. "Indeed! How the hell are ya, woman?"

"I'm great! Things are good."

"Good, I'm glad. How's my brother treating ya?"

"Like gold, as always. I want to hear all about your drama, but I have some news of my own. Who goes first?"

"It is not my drama," Anna pouted.

"Uh huh." Toni snorted out a laugh.

"Shut up. You go first, then. Tell me your news. Let me guess. Promotion at work already?"

"Nope."

"Um… you're pregnant."

Toni paused for a second, then said happily, "Yup."

Anna bolted to sit upright on her bed. "WHAT?"

Toni giggled.

"I was joking! Are you joking?"

"Nope. We were going to call you tonight, actually. We're going to start telling everyone, but Gavin and I agreed we wanted you to be the very first to know." Toni's voice softened with affection. "Because you're the reason we met. You're the one who pushed us together when we were too shy to act on it. So… yes, you're going to be an auntie again. I'm knocked up."

"Ahhhh!" Anna shrieked. "Oh my God, I'm so happy for you both! Oh my God. Oh my God!"

Toni laughed.

"I love you so much," Anna said, feeling her eyes well up. "Oh, Toni. Awww!"

"Aw, honey, I love you too."

"When are you due?"

"May eighteenth."

"I'm going to come visit in June, then!" Anna jumped off her bed, pacing her tiny room in excitement. "Oh my goodness. Are you going to find out what you're having?"

"Yes," Toni said. "Gavin has to know. I'm fine with that."

"Typical doctor," Anna muttered jokingly. "He has to know everything. So I'm really the first to know?"

"Yup! I hit thirteen weeks yesterday, so now we'll tell the world."

"How are you feeling?"

"Better now. I had morning sickness and all that fun, but now it's passed and I'm feeling so much better."

"Aww, ya poor thing. I'm glad you're better." A thought struck Anna. "I'm going to Long Island for Thanksgiving with Sean, Cass, and the girls. Tell Gavin he has to reach Sean by then, because I won't be able to keep this to myself. I'm too happy."

"I'll tell him." Toni laughed. "I'll make sure he calls him tonight."

They talked for a while about the whole McKinnon clan, catching each other up on family tidbits and gossip. When Toni said, "Okay, enough about everyone else. Let's talk about you," Anna flopped back down onto her bed with a sigh.

"You're the one I needed to talk to about this," Anna said.

"Why?"

"Because I'm thinking this is something like how you felt when you hooked up with Gavin and got scared and kept pushing him away. Because you didn't trust it, or that a man like him would really be interested in you."

"Damn, girl. Hit it right on the head. Yeah, we need to talk," Toni said. "So is this where I tell you something like what you told me—tell you what an idiot you're being because you're fabulous, beautiful, smart, and a power-house?"

"Cassandra did that already," Anna said. "Doesn't seem to have sunk in."

"Oh man. So let's take this from a different angle. Tell me more about David."

Anna paused, her mind spinning out as she thought of him. "David… is sooo not my type."

"We've established that. And you're not his. You like each other anyway."

"Yeah, we have amazing sex, and he's nice to me."

"That's not what I said. Focus."

Anna laughed. "Right. Yes, we seem to like each other beyond that. I mean…" Anna reached up and twirled the ends of her hair around her finger. The ends were still magenta and orange. The day after Thanksgiving, she'd dye them different colors for the Christmas season. She loved playing with colors according to seasons and holidays. Last year she'd done red and green. Maybe this year, she'd just do red. Or could she do silver? She wondered what David would think. She had a feeling he'd like whatever she decided to do to it. Which was kind of incredible, considering his world.

"Hello?" Toni asked.

"He likes my crazy hair," Anna said. "And my tattoos. He drops teeny tiny kisses on my nose stud. He licks my tats when we're in bed. TMI?"

"Of course not. Go on."

"At first, I thought we were just kind of... fascinated with each other. Because we're just so different. Along with the instant chemistry, I mean. Like, we kept going back for more because the sex was so great. Who needs more of a reason than that?"

"I sense a 'but' coming," Toni said.

"But... I really like him. He says he likes me too. We're... we've got this yin and yang thing going. And it actually works. So far, anyway." Anna rolled onto her side to stare out her one small window. The sky outside was a clear blue, no clouds, bright sunshine. "I think I bring fun into his world, and he... he kind of brings... he's a very... solid presence. But I *like* that. He's no nonsense. He's intense and kind of serious but has this dry sense of humor and he's so damn smart it's kind of intimidating and he touches my

127

body like he worships it and treats me with respect even when he's pulling my hair in bed and I just really like him." She took a deep breath.

"Wow," Toni said. "I'm hearing nothing but good things here. So... the problem is? Let's pinpoint it. It's not still Ethan, is it? Thought you were well past all that."

"I am..." Anna closed her eyes and sighed. Rolled over to her other side. Twirled her hair around her fingertips. "The problem is Christopher," she finally murmured.

"Ahhhh, now we're getting somewhere," Toni said. "I thought it, but wanted you to get there on your own."

"I got there on the first night with David—are you kidding?" Anna sighed again and pulled up her comforter to cover her legs. "Christopher has been in the back of my mind the whole time."

"David is not Christopher," Toni said.

"I know."

"I don't think you do."

"They're too much alike."

"You're not being fair. To David, or to yourself. You have to try."

"That's probably what I'd say to you," Anna admitted. "You're good at this advice stuff."

"That's right. So listen to me and *hear* me. David is his own man. Christopher was an *asshole*."

"Fully aware."

"Right. So don't let that asshole rent another day of

space in your head. He's had too many already. Evict that stupid bastard once and for all."

Anna blew out a long, slow breath. "It's hard, Toni."

"I know, honey," Toni said softly. "I know. I've been where you are. Which is why I'll help you fight it and have this conversation with you as many times as you need me to."

"Thanks," Anna whispered. "I might take you up on that."

"Go right ahead. I love you. I'm always here for you, even though I'm far away."

"I know. That's why I texted you last night."

"I'm glad you did. Keep doing that."

BY THE TIME David got to the bar, it was close to ten-thirty. He'd worked late, then wolfed down two slices of pizza at the place around the corner from his office. The day had been stressful and crazed, as days before a holiday usually were. He was tired, he hadn't packed for the trip home yet, and half of him wanted to just fall into bed.

The other half of him needed to see Anna. He hadn't in three days, but as short a time as that was, he missed her. Before they both went their separate ways for Thanksgiving, he wanted to see her again.

Sean and Jimmy, the owners of the bar, favored classic rock, so tonight it was the sounds of Led Zeppelin that greeted him as he pulled open the door to O'Reilly's. David wasn't surprised to see that the bar was packed, since Anna had told him it always was on the night before Thanksgiving. But this was more than packed; he could barely make his way through the wall-to-wall crowd. It was louder than usual, the cacophony of voices rising over the music. There was a different energy tonight, something palpable. Maybe it was the holiday season kicking into full swing. Whatever it was, David could feel it, a pulse through the room like a heartbeat. There was something edgy about it.

Anna was behind the bar, in her usual work outfit: all black clothes and her hair in its ponytail. He loved pulling that elastic out when she came over, running his fingers through the silky strands as it fell to her shoulders. Sandwiched between the other two bartenders, she laughed at something the taller one said as she grabbed a pint glass and filled it.

David watched her work. He liked watching her work. When she was behind the bar, with that barrier between her and the world, she was in her element. Comfortable, highly competent, empowered, and gorgeous. He liked watching her gauge the crowd, how those bright blue eyes would scan the scene quick as lightning to see who needed what next. He admired her efficiency in getting out drinks as fast as possible, her concentration as she worked, and loved her smiles that could brighten up a dark night.

She was smart, capable, charismatic, and strong. Why

was she wasting all that raw talent behind a bar night after night? David couldn't figure that one out. The two times he'd approached the subject, she'd changed it in a heartbeat. It seemed the topic was off-limits. But one day, he'd bring it up again.

For now, they were just dating, and he wanted to enjoy her.

He gently shoved and worked his way through the crowd until he got a spot at the bar in front of her. "Hey."

"Hey yourself!" Her wide smile was bright and genuine. Those blue, blue eyes of hers lit up, making his insides go warm.

He had to shout to be heard. "This place is nuts. You weren't kidding."

"Told ya it would be." She slapped a coaster down. "What'll it be, handsome?"

"Actually, I'm thinking I might not stay long," he said. "You're really busy."

"That's fine." She reached out and squeezed his hand. "It's nice to see you, though. Didn't think I would 'til Saturday."

"I know. I, um…" He smiled softly, held her gaze with his. "I just really wanted to see you before then. Wanted to see your face. So, here I am. And I have, and I'll let you get back to work. I'll come by here on Saturday night, as we discussed. And we'll text each other in the meantime. Have a happy Thanksgiving, Anna."

She looked at him for a long beat, then scooted up over the bar, grabbed his tie to pull him in, and kissed him hard on the mouth.

The patrons around them broke into hoots, wolf whistles, and cheers.

"Hey, gorgeous," a guy said, "can I get a kiss too?"

David's blood turned to fire in his veins. It amazed him how quickly jealousy and possessiveness seared through him. He wasn't a violent man, but he wanted to tear that guy's face off.

But Anna laughed it off and said, "Nope." She kissed David again, then once more before she slid back down to stand behind the bar. "Only my guy gets my kisses."

"Damn right," David murmured. The ire instantly evaporated and morphed into affection. He stared at her and asked, "So does that mean we're exclusive now? Am I your guy?"

"Aren't you?" she said. Her tone was flippant, but her eyes spoke a different story. That flash of vulnerability was back. She was a study in contrasts.

He leaned in and touched her cheek. "Yeah. I am."

Chapter Eleven

"I T'S SO GOOD to have you home," Susan said to her son, smiling warmly at him. She sat on one end of the couch, her knees tucked under her and her cup cradled in her perfectly manicured hands.

"Thanks." David sat at the other end, his posture relaxed as he smiled back at her. "It's good to have a long weekend. I needed the break."

"We're going to be in Boca for Christmas week," she said. "Staying with Judy and Arthur."

"I know."

"Why don't you come down for a few days?"

"Thanks, but I don't think so."

"Just to take a break, get away."

"No, Mom. But thank you." David reached for his mug on the glass coffee table.

"You need some recharge time," she said. "Everyone does."

"Can't argue with that," he replied. "I'm going skiing in the middle of January."

"Oh really? Where?"

"Aspen. Going with a few friends from college."

"Which ones?"

"Jay, Steven, and Cody."

"Nice!" Mom smiled. "You'll have a great time. How long?"

"Just four days. Wrapping it around a weekend." David took another sip of coffee before setting his mug back on the table. Early morning sunlight streamed through the den curtains, washing over the framed photos on the bookshelves, the dark brown patterned carpet, the cream-colored couch and love seat. Jellybean, the gray cat his parents had gotten when he left for college, was slower in her old age. She lay on the tiny bed by the windows, as she had been for over an hour, bathing in the sunlight.

David yawned and scrubbed a hand over his stubbled jaw. Jellybean had the right idea. He'd taken an early train to get out to Jersey, and he wouldn't mind a nap himself. But it was Thanksgiving morning, and tons of cooking ahead. "What will you need help with in the kitchen?"

"I'll let you know, don't you worry." She sipped her coffee. "But thanks in advance."

"Of course."

"Your brother should be here around noon."

David had to smile. When his mom said "your brother", she actually meant Jacob, his wife, and the kids. But Jacob was her baby and always would be. "Okay."

"Are you dating at all?" she asked.

David had to give her props for always being direct. That was how Susan Beren rolled. The question was, should he answer her truthfully? Anna's naked, tattooed body flashed in his mind.

"You paused." Mom's dark eyes widened as she leaned in a drop. "Is there someone, honey?"

David took a deep, cleansing breath. He hadn't planned on telling his parents he was seeing Anna. Mostly because it was still new, and he wasn't ready to share her, or any details about their budding relationship, with the world. Or, at least, that's what he'd told himself. But now as he looked around the elegant furnishings of his parents' den, a dark, sticky truth bubbled up and saturated his gut. Chances were good that his parents wouldn't be thrilled about his dating a tattooed bartending college dropout. They'd be shocked. And even disappointed. That thought made him uneasy, and a little mad too.

"David?" His mother looked at him with a glimmer of hope in her eyes.

"I'm seeing someone," he conceded. "But it's not serious. Not... not yet, anyway. We're still... getting to know each other."

"Ah." Her lips twisted in a sardonic, knowing grin. "So you're just sleeping together."

A shocked laugh burst out of him. "Um, yes, there's that, but it's more than that. Kind of. I mean..."

"I know how private you are. I won't push." She leaned

back, but her stare didn't let him loose.

That expectant stare always broke him and made him talk. Like he was still a kid. "She's smart and nice and fun," he said. "And really gorgeous. How's that for now?"

"I'll take it. If it turns into more, you'll tell me?"

"Let me get there first, Mom."

"Okay." She sipped her tea. "Jewish?"

"No. Irish. Like, from Ireland, still has some of the accent. But she's lived in New York for almost a decade now."

"Interesting. Must be lovely to listen to her talk. I love Irish accents."

David looked at his mother for a long beat, his brain churning. "Can I ask you something? Strictly between us?"

Her smile faded. "Of course. You know if you ask me that, I'm a vault."

"Yeah, I do." He leaned forward to grasp his mug again, sipped his coffee as thoughts crashed around in his head. "I think I know the answer to this, but I'm going to ask you anyway."

"Okay. Shoot."

"How important is it to you that I end up with a Jewish girl?"

She blinked, clearly taken aback by his question. "David. Honey. Would it be nice just because it'd be easier for you both, being from the same background? Sure. Is it a must for me? No. I don't care who you end up with, as long as she treats you like gold. That's all that matters to me."

He nodded, leaning his elbows on his knees. "I thought you'd say that." He gave a long, hard look as he asked, "But what about Dad?"

She pursed her lips, and David thought, *Damn*.

"Well…" she said carefully, "I won't lie. He'd like to see you end up marrying someone Jewish. Yes. But it's not his life, it's yours. And, if the woman in question is wonderful, I'm pretty sure he'll get over that quickly." She peered at him. "Ultimately, he just wants you to be happy, honey. We both do. That's all that really matters, to both of us. I thought you knew that."

"I do." But he sighed. It was easy to push this aside in the city, where his life was his own and he was on his own. But now, being back in the house he'd grown up in, with his parents and soon to be surrounded by more family… would it really be okay with them if he brought someone like Anna home? He wasn't sure, and he hated that.

He hated that anything Anna had ever said, or even just implied, could be right.

He turned the mug in slow circles on the tabletop. Not meeting his mother's eyes, he said, "What if I brought home someone who didn't finish college, worked as a bartender, and had a lot of tattoos? Still okay?"

Mom's mouth rounded for a few seconds. Then she recovered and said firmly, "Is she good to you?"

"Yes," he said.

Mom's head moved in a long, slow nod. "Then okay."

"Seriously?" He shot her a skeptical look.

"Yeah, seriously. It's your life, David." She balanced her mug in the cradle of her palms. "Don't ever let me, Dad, or *anyone* make you question your choices about your private life. Do what makes you happy. Find someone who makes you happy. Find someone…" She searched for the words. "Find someone who when you're with them, you feel like you're home. I don't mean *here*." She gestured around the room, meaning the house. "I mean, you feel like *that person* is your home. Whether it's this woman, or someone else. That's the goal. Okay?"

He stared at her, affection and respect welling in his chest. "Yeah, Mom. Thanks."

"You got it." She nodded and sipped her coffee. "But now I have to ask. Tattoos? Really?"

He laughed softly. "A bunch."

"Are they nice ones, at least?"

"Fantastic," he murmured. "Like her."

David: *Happy Thanksgiving.*

Anna: *Back at u! How's the family, how's NJ?*

David: *Fine & fine. Same as always. How's LI?*

Anna: *Same as always.*

David: *Do you even care at all about this holiday? You didn't grow up with it, so I'm just curious.*

Anna: *It's a good excuse to not have to work & to eat a lot.*

So I'm on board

David: *LOL. Okay.*

Anna: *There's a bunch of women in the kitchen. They won't let me help. Insisted I'm a guest, even though I've been here several times now. So I'm hanging out w/ my nieces & my brother*

David: *What are you doing with them? Video games?*

Anna: *No, they're too wee for that. First we took them for a walk outside. Now Sean is trying to get Ella (the baby) down for a nap. I'm with Rose (the 5 y/o) & we're playing Candy Land*

David: *Oh wow. I remember that game. Good stuff.*

David: *You called them "wee". That's adorable, my Irish lass.*

Anna: *I'm a lot of things, but I'm not adorable*

David: *Hate to break it to you, but you kind of are. And yes, lots of other things too.*

Anna: *Like what?*

David: *You want a list of your attributes?*

Anna: *Yes*

David: *Surely you're well aware of them by now. You're just looking for compliments.*

Anna: *Yes*

David: *LOL*

David: *You're drop-dead gorgeous, but you know that. Sexy as hell. A goddess in bed.*

Anna: *Wow*

Anna: *What else?*

David: *Ha! Well…*

David: *The even better stuff. You're smart. Strong. Kind. You take risks.*

David: *Have a good work ethic. A mush around kids. Love your family. Have a salty mouth.*

David: *And put up with my insane work schedule.*

Anna: *Well, u put up with mine too. #VampireHours*

David: *Did you hear anything else I said, woman?*

Anna: *Yes. U love my salty mouth. Remind me to drop F-bombs more often*

David: *Okay sure but HOW ABOUT THE OTHER STUFF?*

Anna: *LOL yes. Yes I did. Thank u very much* ☺

Anna: *In fact, my head is now too huge to get through the door*

David: *I meant every word.*

Anna: *Thank u. Really xxx*

David: *Triple X? Like a porn rating?*

Anna: *LOL!!!*

Anna: *Those are kisses, fool*

David: *Just checking.*

"So, Dave," Jacob said as he passed the mashed sweet potatoes to his wife. "Tell us about this mystery woman you're dating."

David glared at his older brother across the table. *Now*, in the middle of the Thanksgiving meal, with all their family sitting there, he was going to do this?

"What?" Jacob asked, trying to look innocent and failing.

"Nope," David snapped, and reached for the bottle of Malbec to top off his wineglass. Clearly, this would be a meal that needed alcoholic reinforcement.

"I want to hear too," Sharon said. "I didn't even know you were dating someone until your mom mentioned it in the kitchen."

David wasn't a big fan of his sister-in-law. She was a decent mother and wife, but she was also pretentious and phony, always looking for gossip. So again, he simply said, "No."

"I didn't even know until today," Susan said, shooting a look at her son that was both apologetic and worried. "None of us did."

"And now I'm regretting I ever said anything," David groused. He felt all the eyes on him now: his parents, his brother and sister-in-law, his two nephews and niece, his aunt and uncle and cousin. He took a gulp of wine. "You can all stare at me all you want. I'm not saying another word about it."

It was his cousin, Marc, who swept in to attempt a rescue. "Maybe Dave doesn't feel like discussing his love life in front of the whole family. Imagine that. The nerve."

David couldn't hold back his grin, and raised his glass in

a toast to Marc before downing another large gulp of Malbec. Only two years younger, Marc had always had his back, since they were kids. "You've always been my favorite cousin."

"Well, I'm your *only* cousin on this side," Marc pointed out, "but thanks."

"You're better than him," David said, gesturing with his glass toward his brother, who promptly looked annoyed.

"That's not hard," Marc joked, smiling widely.

"Ooh, burrrrrrn," said Brandon, Jacob's older son. The eleven-year-old snickered.

Jacob shot his son a hard warning look before saying to David, "You can't blame us for being curious. You never bring anyone you date home, talk about anyone—"

"And I'm also not talking about this now," David replied. "Possibly ever." He looked down the table at his mother. "Dinner's great. Everything's wonderful. Thank you. And next time... please. C'mon."

Mom pursed her lips and said quietly, "Sorry, honey. It slipped out. I was talking to Aunt Barbra and I just—"

"It's okay. Let's move on." David gave her a tight smile and took another sip.

His father leaned toward his mother and said, "I'd like to hear about this..."

"Later, Howard," she hissed. She looked down the table toward her three grandchildren. "So! How's school, kids?"

David enjoyed the rest of the meal, along with half the

bottle of Malbec. So he was fairly relaxed an hour later when the men went into the den to watch some football. Marc flopped down on the shorter couch beside him. His dad, his uncle, and Jacob took the longer couch. They all watched the game in amiable silence for two minutes before David murmured, "Thanks for the save before."

"Anytime." Marc winced at the play onscreen before whispering, "So is it serious?"

"What?"

"You and the mystery woman."

"No. It's only been a few weeks. Which is why it's not up for discussion."

"You told your mom," Marc said with a snort. "How long did you think that would stay quiet?"

David rolled his eyes and blew out a harried breath. "Thought that shit ended in my twenties."

"It'll never end until you get married, *bubela*," Marc joked.

"Wonderful."

Uncle Gary groaned aloud at the screen. "Pass the damn ball! Come ON!"

"They suck," his dad proclaimed. "Jesus, this is ridiculous."

"I'm going to lose some money on this game," Jacob growled.

David felt his cell phone vibrate in his jeans pocket and pulled it out.

Anna: Hey, handsome. What r u doing?

David: Watching football with the menfolk and being bored. Slouching through my food coma. You're saving me.

Anna: I'm good like that

David: Very good. What are you up to out on the Island?

Anna: Post-meal food comas here too. In the basement, which has play area for the kids. I currently have a half-asleep kindergartener on my lap. Toddler is roaming around the room

Anna: Since I'm not allowed to help in the kitchen w anything, I've been designated the babysitter. I'm fine w that, I love my girls. We're watching Frozen

David: The Disney flick?

Anna: Yes. They're little girls, it's the law to watch that like every day

David: I have a young niece, I understand.

Anna: I was thinking about u

David: Oh yeah? Something dirty, I hope.

Anna: Very dirty

David: Mmmm. Clue me in. Give me a visual to get through the rest of this evening.

Anna: I thought you liked being w ur family?

David: I usually do... just annoyed at my brother right now.

Anna: What'd he do? Throw turkey at u? Deny u pumpkin pie?

David: LOL, no. He asked me about you. In front of the entire family. During the meal. Good times.

David: …hello?

Anna: U told ur brother about me?

David: No. Told my mom. Who apparently then told everyone else. Thanks, Mom.

Anna: U told ur mom about us??

David: Yes. Is that a problem?

Anna: No. I'm just surprised

David: She asked if I'd met anyone, as usual. This time, I told her yes I have. That's all.

Anna: That's all?

David: What else should I have told her?

Anna: I don't know

David: Oh wait. I forgot. I then told her how you love it when I take you hard up against the wall, and how I love when you get on top and ride me like a cowgirl.

Anna: You. Did. Not.

David: She was riveted. She cheered for me.

Anna: LOL!!!

David: She gave me a case of condoms as an early Hanukkah gift & told me to keep having fun.

Anna: OMG ur mad. MAD!

David: No, huh?

Anna: Ur wicked! I can't stop laughing

David: Well, good.

David: All I told her was I met a beautiful woman, we've been seeing each other, and I like her. That's all she needs to know. Or she'd have us married and our kids named before dessert.

Anna: Aha. Okay then

David: I'm fairly private when it comes to my personal life, Anna. I'm close to my family, but I'm not the type to dish about my love life with my family. Just saying.

Anna: All good, Suit

David: I love it when you call me that. So romantic.

Anna: It's better than calling you "wanker"

David: True. Very true. Thanks for that.

Anna: LOL

David: Well hey, your brother knows about us, so now both families know. Kind of.

Anna: He's kind of known all along, yes

David: What does that mean?

Anna: Um… that 1st morning I left ur place? He actually caught me doing the walk of shame. I ran into him around the corner from ur place

Anna: Him, of all people! So yeah, he's kinda known from Day One

David: HAHAHAHAHA

Anna: YOU SHUT UP MISTER!!

David: HAHAHAHAHA

Anna: I'm gonna smack u so hard when I see u

David: Oooh, promise?

Anna: *Ur naughty*

David: *I miss you, gorgeous.*

Anna: *Awww. I miss u too*

DAVID GOT TO O'Reilly's Tavern at eight. It was earlier than he'd planned, but he couldn't stay away any longer. He'd missed Anna and wanted to see her. Even if she was working, he could think of worse ways to spend a Saturday night than sitting in a cool bar, having a few drinks, and watching a sexy, beautiful woman do her thing.

He just wanted to look at her. It was that simple.

The bar was busy when he walked in, the scene in its usual noisy chaos. He realized that in the handful of weeks he'd been seeing Anna, he'd spent more time hanging out at a bar than he had since his mid-twenties. Back then, it'd been hanging out late with co-workers to blow off the steam of stressful, high-octane days. He liked this much better.

David made his way through the crowd and right up to the polished mahogany bar. As he now knew was the usual for a Saturday night, there were three bartenders working instead of two. He didn't recognize the third one tonight, a guy in his late twenties, but he gestured a quick hello to John before catching Anna's eye.

When she saw him, her face changed. Her eyes widened a drop, her cheeks got a bit rosy, and her smile rivaled midday sunshine. Her obvious happy reaction to seeing him made his insides go all warm and fuzzy.

"Hey!" she said, unable to wipe the goofy smile off her face. She reached out to grab his hand and squeezed it. "Hi! You're a little earlier than I expected."

"What can I say, I wanted to see you," he said, feeling his own smile go wide.

"That's nice to hear. But I don't get off work 'til one A.M.," she said. "You're really gonna hang around here for that long?"

"Maybe," he said. His eyes traveled over her. "It's good to see you, Anna. You look gorgeous."

"It's good to see you too." She leaned in closer, her eyes twinkling with a sudden spark of mischief. "I want to be alone with you. Are we in bed yet, dammit?"

He laughed. "Soon. Not soon enough, but very soon."

"Oh good."

"Get back to work."

"Yes, sir." She grabbed a pint glass from beneath the bar. "Want a Julius to start?"

"That sounds great."

He watched her eyes linger on him for a few seconds before she turned away to get him his drink. She was glowing because he was there. It made him smile back as something twinged in his chest.

SHAFTS OF SUNLIGHT warmed Anna's face. Barely opening

her eyes, she looked over at David beside her, who was sound asleep. His dark stubble was heavier along his jaw, highlighting his full lips. She ran her fingertip over them with a feather's touch. She loved the shape of them, the feel of them. She gazed at him for a few more seconds, then carefully got out of bed and tiptoed to the bathroom to relieve herself.

As she padded down the short hallway, the cooler air of the apartment hit her, making her suck in a breath. The wood floor was cold beneath her bare feet. She took care of business, quickly rinsed her mouth out with mouthwash, then practically sprinted back to bed. She curled up into David's warm, firm body, savoring both the warmth beneath the covers and the delicious feel of him.

He groaned and shifted his legs. "Ah shit!" His deep voice was thick with sleep. "Your feet are freezing."

She chuckled but moved them away from him. "Sorry, love."

He gave a little grunt, but his strong arms slid around her, holding her closer. "It's okay. C'mere. Just not your feet. Leave them on the floor."

She giggled as she nestled into his embrace. He was warm and his hair was all mussed and he looked both sexy as hell and sweetly adorable. The dark hair on his chest tickled her cheek. Running her hand over his bicep, she dropped a kiss on his skin and closed her eyes to go back to sleep.

But his hips nudged her, and she felt his growing erection against her belly.

"Some parts of you are more awake than others," she whispered.

David cleared his throat. "Around you, that part of me is pretty much always awake."

She smiled and said, "I have noticed that."

His mouth sought hers, kissing her sweetly. "Good morning."

"Good morning."

"What time is it?"

"Half past seven."

He groaned in protest. "We need more sleep."

"Yes."

"But I'm going to ravish you again when we wake up later."

"Sounds good to me."

He kissed her again, lingering on her lips. "I like waking up with you," he whispered. "Wish we could do it more often." His eyes, heavy with sleep, opened halfway to look into hers. She marveled for the hundredth time at the gold flecks in the pools of hazel. "I missed you, Anna."

She smiled and kissed him. "Same here, on all counts."

"Then you should sleep over more often."

"I should, huh?"

"Yes." He gazed at her intently. "Yes, you should."

She kissed him again. "Maybe I will."

"Good." He smiled as his eyes closed. His arms tightened

around her. "Back to sleep for us."

She closed her eyes too as she nestled into him again. Drawing a long, cleansing breath, she enjoyed their warm, entangled limbs, the feel of his body aligned with hers, the cozy warmth of their cocoon under his thick comforter... it was a sweet, romantic, perfect moment like she hadn't had in a long time, and she relished it. She let herself drown in it.

Chapter Twelve

"WELL, NOW THAT I'm more caffeinated," Anna said, "I'm going to tell you what I'd like to do today. You won't want to do it, but I really really want to, so I hope you'll indulge me and say yes."

David shot her a sideways glance, then speared another forkful of his scrambled eggs. "Well, you don't know that for sure. Hit me."

The sounds of the small café filled the air around them. Anna was secretly glad David had dragged her out for brunch, both because after a morning round of sex in his shower she was starving, and that it had gotten them outside. She could have been very easily tempted to stay in bed with this man all day. She took another bite of her whole wheat toast before wiping her hands on her napkin and launching into it.

"I want to go see the tree at Rockefeller Center as soon as it gets dark," she said.

"Whaaat?" His dark brows lifted in protest. "On the Sunday right after the tree went up? Are you nuts? It'll be a zoo."

"I know. That's part of the fun of it." She smiled, sensing she needed to pour on some extra charm. "I do it every year. It's a fun way to kick off the holidays."

"Oh, you mean this wasn't it?" He grinned and reached across the table to fiddle with a lock of her hair, rubbing the newly dyed red streaks between his fingers. Some of the ends in the front, framing her face, were tipped in green. Her earrings were red Christmas lights. "You're like a walking billboard for Christmas. You could be an elf at Macy's or something."

She laughed. "Well, yeah, that too. But c'mon. Please come with me. It'll be fun, I promise."

He shoveled another forkful of eggs into his mouth, chewing and swallowing before nodding. "Sure. That's what you want to do later, why not. But what about the rest of the afternoon until then?"

"Um... I need to do some shopping for holiday gifts," Anna said. "My nieces, my brother and sister-in-law... Could we do some of that?"

"Not my favorite thing in the world, but yeah, we could do that. I have to get a few gifts too, for my brother's kids and my parents, so—" His cell phone rang and he glanced at the screen. A small, warm grin bloomed on his face. "Speak of the devil." He lifted the phone to his ear and said, "Hi, Mom. How are you?"

Trying not to show her interest in David's conversation, Anna made a show of finishing her acai bowl and not making eye contact with him.

"Yeah, I'm out at brunch right now," he said as he fidgeted with his fork. "Can I call you back tonight? Oh. Right. Well, have a good time… yeah, actually, I did forget. Just had a crazy busy week at work and…" He looked at Anna and made a face like, "Sorry!"

She gestured to him with a "No worries, it's fine" wave.

"Mom. Mom… yeah, sorry, I have to go. I'm with someone, so this is rude… ummm, yes actually. Yes, I am." He looked pointedly at Anna.

She realized that look meant his mother had asked if he was with *that woman he'd been seeing*. She made a face as if to say, "eeeeek!"

He nodded, shooting a wry grin as he said to his mom, "Yes, she is… we are… I'll tell her. Yup. Okay. Happy Hanukkah to you too. Tell Dad I said hi, and I'll talk to you soon. Okay… love you too. Bye." He put down the phone and said, "Sorry about that."

"Don't be, it's fine." Anna smiled. "You're nice to your mother. You sound like you have a good relationship. I like that."

"She's a wonderful woman," David said. "A fantastic mom. I'm lucky."

"That's lovely." Anna bit down on her lip. "Um… did Hanukkah start?"

"Not 'til Wednesday night," he said. "But my mom knows how busy I get during the week and that she might

154

not talk to me on the first night, so she was just covering her bases." He grinned and reached for his coffee cup.

"I *thought* it started on Wednesday night this year," she said. "That's why I was asking. I got confused."

He stared at her. "You're keeping track of when Hanukkah starts, my Irish lass?"

Anna felt herself blush slightly, but she only nodded. "This year, aye, I am."

"And why would you do that?"

"Because the guy I'm dating is a nice Jewish boy, and I should know when his holiday starts."

David let out a chuckle. "Well, I'm all *verklempt*."

She shrugged, but her heart rate had risen. "I, uh... hope you don't think I'm being disingenuous. I'm not trying to... I don't know, be weird about it. I just—"

"I know, Anna." His hand slid across the tabletop to intertwine his fingers with hers. "That's really nice," he said quietly, squeezing her hand. "I'm touched."

They gazed at each other and smiled.

"So," Anna asked, "what did your mom want you to tell me?"

David's eyes went down to their hands as he quirked a wry grin. "That she hopes you're not too sore from whatever I did to you last night."

"She did *not*," Anna insisted, laughing. "Tell me whatever she really said."

He huffed out a laugh. "Just that she hopes you and I

have a nice day together."

"Why was that hard to tell me?"

"It wasn't. I just like to keep you on your toes."

"Well, you certainly do that."

"Do I?" He looked surprised. "I wasn't sure. You're a pretty sharp woman."

"You do," she assured him. "And it's one of the things I like most about you."

"Back atcha," he said, and winked.

"THIS IS HELL on earth," David groused. He held on tightly to Anna's hand so he wouldn't lose her in the crowd. "Why are we here again?"

"Christmas spirit," Anna declared.

"Bah humbug." David tried to stick close to her. He couldn't believe the sheer volume of people at Rockefeller Center. The NYPD had put up metal gates, about waist high, to try to make some lines and bring order to the chaos. A few cops stood together, watching over the crowd. Damn, there were a lot of people on the street. All to see a Christmas tree. He couldn't get over it. "You'd think none of these people have ever seen a Christmas tree before. I mean, this is insanity. What the hell?"

"Don't rain on my parade, Suit," Anna warned him.

He blew out a breath. She was right. This meant something to her, and he didn't want to ruin it for her. "Sorry, babe. It's just there's a *lot* of people here."

"I know. You're fine." She gave him a quick smile and a kiss on the lips, then kept leading the way through the crowd.

It was dark already and it was only a quarter to five. Even with the noise of the crowd, David could vaguely make out Christmas music playing somewhere nearby. They got a little bit further along… and then, there it was. The famous majestic, towering tree, covered in colorful lights, standing tall.

"Ohhhh." Anna stared up at it, utterly enchanted. "Isn't it beautiful?"

David looked down at her and smiled at the childlike wonder and joy on her face. "Yes." Standing behind her, his arms snaked around her waist to hold her close. Her puffy silver coat was soft under his gloved hands. The ruby-red hat she wore was softer than it looked, rubbing against his jaw. She looked both too cool to be there with him, and totally sexy-slash-adorable. People jostled them slightly, but he held her tight as they looked up at the tree together.

"The tree is beautiful, but…" He leaned down and said in her ear, "You're *more* beautiful, you know."

"Awww, sweet talker." But she smiled and rested the back of her head against his chest, squeezing his hands with hers where they were locked around her middle. Then she took her phone out of her bag to snap some pictures of the tree. She made him laugh as they took selfies with the tree in the background.

They stood there for a while. The air was cold, around forty degrees. The sounds of the crowd and Christmas music from who knew where... all of it was loud and the whole scene was barely controlled chaos. But he had to admit that the tree was truly a lovely sight, as well as the many other decorations all around. Anna was glowing with happiness. David just focused on her, the tree, and being in the moment. Too much of his world was busy, always go-go-go, working too many hours... Sweetness like this moment was something rare, and pure, and he was affected. It surprised him, how much he was enjoying it.

"You're special," he murmured against her cheek.

"I'm sorry, what?" she said, straining to hear him over the noise around them.

"You're special," he said, "and I'm glad to be here with you."

She turned in his arms to look into his eyes. He kept his arms around her waist as hers slid up to lock around his neck. Her smile was soft and pleased. "I'm glad to be here with you too." She leaned in to seal her mouth to his. They stood and kissed as the people and sounds and colors and lights swirled all around them.

~

Anna: *Hey, Suit. Whassup, hottie?*

David: *Hi gorgeous. Crazy busy at work. The usual.*

Anna: *Can u come out to play tonight? There's something I'd like to show u*

David: *I've seen it.*

Anna: *Ha. Ha. Ha.*

David: *It's Wednesday. Aren't you working tonight?*

Anna: *I took the night off. Because I really wanted to see u and show u this thing. Please say yes*

David: *Wow. Okay. Yes.*

Anna: *Oh good. Need u to meet me at 5:00, no later than 5:15. Can u?*

David: *I'll make it happen. I can meet you somewhere if that saves time. Give me an address.*

Anna: *Meet me in front of Carnegie Hall, on the W 57th St side*

David: *Hmmm. The plot thickens. Are you taking me to a concert? Didn't know you liked classical music.*

Anna: *No concert. Just meeting there. It's a surprise*

David: *A top secret surprise, huh?*

Anna: *Yes. Not a big deal, mind u, but a holiday surprise*

David: *We already went and saw the tree, shopped at FAO Schwartz, and had drinks at McSorley's Pub because you said it was a tradition. What's next, hanging out with Santa and some elves?*

Anna: *Not even close, hotshot. Go work. Ttyl*

$\sim$

IT TOOK SOME doing and serious task-shifting, but at five

o'clock sharp, David waited on the corner of West 57th Street and Seventh Avenue as Anna had instructed him to. He glanced up at Carnegie Hall, decorated for the holidays but otherwise architecturally unremarkable. His mother and grandmother had taken him and his brother to a few concerts here when they were kids, so David knew the inside of the building was much more impressive than the outside. Those trips held good memories.

This was a nice part of the city, somewhat quieter than midtown, and one David hadn't spent a lot of time in. He stood under a lamppost so Anna could see him easily, his hands in the pockets of his long wool overcoat. The night air wasn't too cold, but chilly enough that he could see his breath in white puffs when he exhaled.

He looked around; most of the buildings and businesses had already been decked out with Christmas decorations. White lights, colored lights, tinsel and garland and brightness everywhere he looked. The lights and sparkle definitely gave the whole city a different feel, more festive and wondrous somehow. And yes, like Anna had said more than once, magical. It had never really had an effect on him before, all this time. But he was appreciating it now. That gorgeous Irish lass was rubbing off on him.

What was she up to with this surprise tonight? A smile played along his lips as he thought of her. Since meeting her, she had also brought light, festivity, and magic into his life. He was grateful for it.

No, he wasn't just grateful. He was falling for her. Hard.

But it gave him pause. They were very different. Would that make it for the long haul? What kind of future could they have together, if he pursued it? Would she fit into his world? Would she even want to?

Something told him she wouldn't want to, but he was in this neck deep anyway.

He exhaled a deep breath, expelling a puffy white cloud that evaporated in front of his eyes. Life was a series of risks, a game of chance. He knew that from work. He'd just never applied the same mindset to romantic relationships. They'd always been easier. Or, no… maybe he just hadn't applied the same guerrilla tactics to women because he liked women.

Then again, he hadn't had tremendous success with relationships. He'd always been too focused on his career, ever since the end of high school. He'd always had one eye on the future, what he needed to accomplish, the next step up the ladder. His romantic life had suffered as a result. Other than Wendy in college, and Kimberly in his late twenties—at least he hadn't married Kimberly, or surely he'd already be divorced by now. But yeah… he wanted something. Something more. He was ready now.

Or maybe, it was just that he wanted something more, specifically, with Anna.

"Hey!" she called out to him as she walked toward him.

He smiled, insides instantly aglow at the sight of her. Dark skinny jeans and colorful army boots, her puffy silver coat, a blue and purple scarf that matched the blue wool hat on her head. She smiled as she reached him, slipping her arms around his neck and pulling his head down for a kiss. Her mouth was warm, soft, giving. He cradled her face in his hands as he deepened the kisses, touching his tongue to hers, sparking little fires throughout his body.

"Your cheeks are cold," he murmured as he kissed her.

"So are your hands," she said. "No gloves, tough guy?"

He laughed. "I forgot them at the office. They're keeping my desk nice and warm."

"That's a shame." She pulled back enough to smile up at him. "Ready to see what I want to show you?"

"A surprise in this area? I'm definitely intrigued." He gave her one more kiss before stepping back, taking her gloved hand in his. It was soft and he gave it a squeeze. "Lead the way."

"I was looking something up," she said as they started to walk down West 57th, "and I came across this. I thought of you immediately, and..." A shy smile crossed her face. "Well, I just hope you like it. Maybe you've seen it a hundred times before, maybe you haven't, I dunno. Just thought that—"

"Thanks for thinking of me," he cut her off, squeezing her fingers in his. "In advance. It's nice to be thought of."

"I think of you all the time," she admitted quietly.

He stopped, tugging her hand to make her stop walking too. "What'd you say?"

Unable to meet his eyes, she gazed at his chin instead. "You heard me."

"You think of me all the time?"

"Um… well not *all* the time. I have other things to think about too. Like how to mix a Fifth Gear. Don't do that drink often enough to remember on my own, so—"

He cradled her face with both hands and cut off her words with a kiss. A deep, searing, passionate yet tender kiss. He pulled back to look into her eyes, leaning his forehead against hers. "I think of you all the time too."

Her breath caught, but she just stared back at him.

"Something's happening here," he whispered. "Between us."

"It's just holiday magic," she said nervously. "People get swept away."

"Okay, then. If you say so." He ran his fingertips along her cheek, never breaking eye contact. "Then I'm swept away. Blame it on the holiday spirit. But there's definitely something changing here. Getting… deeper. I feel it. I think you do too."

She licked her lips and swallowed. "Maybe."

He gazed deeper into her eyes. What was she afraid of? He needed to find out. He needed to get her to open up to him about whatever was holding her back, because it was obvious that something was.

But not right that second. That was for another time. He kissed her again, long and sweet. "Show me the surprise," he said, pulling back and taking her hand again.

They walked east for two more blocks, then she pulled him to turn onto Fifth Avenue. There was the grand Plaza Hotel, a crowd of people gathered in front of it... and the biggest menorah David had ever seen in his life. "What the...?"

"Surprise!" Anna said with an excited smile. She looked up at the menorah, then back to him. "It's the biggest menorah in the world! That's what the *Guinness World Records* book says. It's thirty-two feet tall! How cool is that?"

David stared up at it, realizing that it was the first night of Hanukkah and he'd totally forgotten. And Anna had remembered and brought him here to see this. He grasped her face and kissed her hard.

"Happy Hanukkah, David," she said when he let her come up for air.

"Thank you, sweetheart." Overcome with emotion, he just stared at her and smiled. He probably looked like a goofy idiot. He was fine with that.

"Have you been here before?" she asked. "Probably like every year, right?"

"No," he said, caressing her cheeks with his thumbs, unwilling to let her go. "No, actually, I haven't. I'm always working. I've never been."

"Never?" Her eyes widened in shock. "But you grew up in New Jersey! The article said they started this, like, in 2005, maybe?"

"Never made it here." He kissed her again, savoring the feel of her soft, warm lips against his. "Thank you for bringing me. This is… this is cool."

"Well, you came with me to see the tree. So I wanted to do something for your holiday too. Holidays in Manhattan are just the best. So I looked online and found this…" She gave a shy, adorable shrug as she smiled at him. Affection and happiness were clear in her beautiful blue eyes. "Because what you said before was true: something's happening here. And I just…" She shrugged again and bit down on her bottom lip. "I wanted to give you a bit of holiday magic too. Because, even though it scares me to say it out loud… you matter to me."

He fell in love with her right there and then.

Chapter Thirteen

Anna smiled as she curled into David's side. He'd liked her surprise of bringing him to the biggest menorah lighting; thankfully, he hadn't thought she was being cheesy or, even worse, disingenuous in any way. He got that she was trying to do something nice for him, to acknowledge his heritage and traditions too. That she was meeting him in the middle, and didn't expect anything they had to be all about her. That she just wanted to do something special for him. The look in his eyes… it was as if she'd handed him a million dollars or something. It took her breath away.

He kept his arm around her waist or held her hand the whole time. As the rabbi climbed into a cherry picker to be lifted up to light the candle—which was really turning a light bulb on, of course—she and David cheered loudly along with the rest of the crowd. The rabbi led the people gathered there in chanting a prayer or two in Hebrew, then the whole crowd sang a few Hanukkah songs.

It moved her, listening to all these people sing their songs. Hearing David sing along had sparked joy in her. He knew the words, sang in Hebrew, and had a sweet smile on his face that showed he was really enjoying himself. A small and simple thing, being there, but it meant something to him.

That made her deeply happy.

Afterward, they had dinner across the street, in the Plaza Hotel. She laughed at first, thinking David was joking, but he insisted. He said he wanted to treat her to a really nice dinner, and that it was his way to celebrate the first night of Hanukkah. How could she say no to him, when he looked all lit up like that?

The grandiose hotel hushed her, making her feel as if she'd walked into a library or a church. Anna had never been inside the Plaza before, and it was as stunning and luxurious as she'd imagined it would be. The marble, the chandeliers, the lavish furnishings... even the people who worked there, or patrons who milled around in the lobby, with its ornate chandeliers and marble floors... it was as if she'd stepped into another world, one more glamorous and beautiful than she belonged to. She felt utterly out of place in such an extravagant setting.

But David... well, especially still in his suit from work, he looked right at home. When she took off her coat, the waiter eyed her and she felt a flicker of his disdain. Her low-cut, skin-tight blue and white top had seemed a great choice initially, but she hadn't thought she'd be going to a super fancy dinner. It revealed a lot of skin; not exactly appropriate in such a high-scale environment. She didn't care, but she didn't want to embarrass David if he cared.

Then a realization hit her with the force of Thor's hammer: she *did* care. She *did* feel more than a little... out of place, and in a way that made her feel lesser than.

But she swallowed it down. Even if she did stick out, her date didn't seem to mind. In fact, David kept gazing at her like she was the only woman in the room, something intense lighting his whiskey eyes. He ordered an obnoxiously expensive fine wine as her eyes skimmed over the menu. Any of the entrees here were usually more than she spent on any *two* meals.

"Are they kidding with these prices?" she muttered.

He glanced at her over the top of his menu. "Problem?"

"Other than being slightly offended by these prices, no."

"Don't look at the prices, then." His deep voice was velvety. "I'm taking you to dinner. You order whatever you want. You hear me?"

"I hear you," she murmured.

He ordered the filet mignon, she ordered shrimp over pasta in some kind of basil pesto sauce, and he made sure her glass was filled before his. As she tasted the Cabernet he'd chosen—good Lord, that was good—she willfully pushed the uncomfortable, unwanted feelings aside. She'd rarely had such an extravagant meal, and she decided to just go on and enjoy it. God knew she'd never go to the Plaza on her own, and the guys she usually dated... safe to say this was *not* their kind of scene.

She stared at David across the table, drinking in his handsome features; he gave her a warm smile and reached for her hand. His long fingers curled around hers and gave them a reassuring, affectionate squeeze. And for a fleeting moment, Anna wondered what a life with him could be like.

Not that he'd ever want to settle down with a woman like her. She knew that. Christopher had made that painfully clear, and she'd never forgotten his scathing words. She was a girl men like them had their fun with, not a girl men got serious with.

But she could wonder and fantasize about being with David... no harm in the fantasies safely locked in her own head.

"You look beautiful," he said.

She smiled in response, her brain churning away.

Not for the first time, she pondered how the old saying of "opposites attract" definitely applied to them. He was quiet, disciplined, had laser focus—the opposite of her, for sure. But it was their differences that made things interesting. He was so locked down; she was such a free spirit. Maybe, in a way, it was that she brought lightness to him, and he kind of... grounded her.

He was so smart and worked incredibly hard, and she respected that. He was *GQ* handsome and sexy in a low, simmering way, which were fantastic bonuses. And oh sweet Lord, he treated her like a queen whenever they were in bed together. The truth was he always treated her well, in and out of bed.

He was good to her. He paid attention, was kind, and made her smile. He liked his family and was fairly close to them. He'd probably make a good father one day…

She gazed at him as he sipped his scotch and he winked at her. Anna felt fizzy inside. She knew she'd fallen for him, hard. Maybe she should clue him in to just how much. Being in a serious relationship with him could be something special, and definitely interesting. She bet she could make him happy, and vice versa, given a real chance. She had to talk to him and see if that was even on his radar, a real relationship.

She swallowed hard, leaned in, and murmured, "David…"

"Yeah, babe?"

Just then, a couple walked past their table. A polished couple in their late fifties, they reeked of money and privilege, and were dressed to the nines. The woman looked down her nose and gave Anna a quick, withering glance that made her feel like a bug on the bottom of a shoe, shaking her back to reality.

This was David's world, not hers. She was a visitor, a girl looking in through the window, and that was all.

"Um…" She swallowed down her desires, her stupid thoughts, her traitorous heart. "I just wanted to thank you for bringing me here."

"It's my pleasure," he said, smiling. He lifted her hand to

his lips and dropped a featherlight kiss on her knuckles, sending shivers up her arm.

The meal was wonderful. After it, they moved to the magnificent lounge for a drink by a roaring fireplace, sitting in velvet wing-backed chairs as others also quietly enjoyed drinks around them. She felt like she was on a movie set, not in real life. The whole evening had had a vaguely magical, surreal feel.

They took a cab back to his apartment. He couldn't keep his hands off her.

"You're amazing," he whispered against her neck as he kissed and nibbled on her skin. His mouth was a wonder, making her shiver with pleasure.

"Why am I amazing?" she whispered back, tipping her head back to give him better access. Her fingers made their way into his thick hair.

"You just are. For a million reasons. Plus you're a sexy goddess." He made his way up the side of her neck to her ear, biting the lobe before sucking it into his hot mouth. His greedy hands made their way into her coat, fondling one breast, then the other, his long fingers pinching her nipples through her sweater, making her breath catch. She felt the warmth spread through her body, pooling between her legs.

"You're giving the cabbie a show," she whispered.

"Shhhh." David sealed his mouth to hers in a hot, hungry kiss.

"I didn't think you were into PDAs," she managed in

between kisses.

"I need to get you home," he murmured against her lips. "I need to be inside you. Like *now*."

Another lustful shiver went down her spine. "Damn, baby."

As soon as they were inside his apartment, he pushed her back against the wall. They tore off each other's coats and ripped at each other's clothes, kissing and groping and grinding. Anna had rarely been so turned on in her life, and that was saying something considering how this man always turned her on.

"Condom?" she said, her voice high and breathy.

"Yeah..." He bent to find his wallet in his pants pocket, tore at the foil. He hitched up her leg, moved her back and up, and thrust into her hard. They both groaned, clutching at each other as they urgently worked each other into a frenzy.

"Christ, you feel so good," she gasped as he pounded into her. She loved this side of him. She loved that she had the power to draw this hungry, passionate beast out of the poised, serious man. The power of that was intoxicating, and she was addicted.

Her name fell from his lips. He took her hard and fast and she clung on to him, her head spinning and every inch of her body on fire. They panted and moaned and rocked together until her orgasm hit like a tidal wave, making her cry out as it swept her away in the dizzying currents. He followed her right over the edge.

They stood there for a minute, holding each other and catching their breath. He smiled at her, those gorgeous hazel eyes filled with obvious affection as he gazed at her, making her heart swell. He kissed her as he carefully withdrew from her body and brought her leg down. "Remember I said you were amazing?" he murmured, gently sweeping her hair back from her face. "You just proved it."

"You're an animal. I loved every second." She smiled and kissed him again.

Half-naked, they went to the kitchen, got glasses of water, gulped them down as they kept smiling at one another. He reached for her hand and led her to his bedroom. Side by side, they stripped off the rest of their clothes and got into his bed, sweaty and spent and thoroughly satisfied.

"Sleep over tonight," he said against her temple, pressing a kiss there. His voice was a deep, sated rumble.

"Is that a command?" she asked lightly.

"A request, madame."

"Aha. That's better."

"But sleep over. Please."

She chuckled against his shoulder as her fingertips played with the dark hair on his chest. She loved the hair on his chest. She adored his body, every inch of it.

"I have to work in the morning, you don't," he said. "I should be the one balking, not you."

A yawn escaped her. "Okay. I'll stay. I'll leave when you

do."

"Good." His arms closed tighter around her, and he sought out her mouth for some languid kisses. "Oh, I meant to tell you…" He kept peppering her lips with kisses. "Friday night, I'll come by the bar to see you, but I'll be really late."

"Okay," she said. Her stomach started to churn. Even though she already knew why, she had to ask or he'd be suspicious. "How come?"

"It's my office holiday party," he said. "No significant others, sorry. But I'm sparing you, believe me. My company party is a bunch of dry or stuck-up suits. You'd hate the whole scene."

She didn't say a word, just nodded against him as her stomach did a full-out flip. She knew she should just say, "I know about the party. I'm working the party. My friend threw me the gig." But for some reason, she couldn't get the words out.

His fingers went under her chin, tipping her face up so he could meet her eyes. "It really is a No-Plus-One policy, Anna. I'm not snubbing you. No spouses or dates allowed— it's like that every year."

"I believe you, David," she said. "No worries." She tried to act completely casual, as though her heart wasn't suddenly pounding faster and her stomach wasn't whirling nauseously. She didn't want him to tell her not to work at his company party. And she wanted the gig; she'd make as much money for that night as she would make in a whole weekend at

O'Reilly's. Now that she was determined to go to Ireland in June, she wanted to book the flight as soon as possible. Holiday spending had cut in on her savings, which were small to begin with, so every extra dollar helped.

Which was something David had never experienced. And that was the truth.

"You'll be at work anyway, right?" he asked.

"Yes," she said. At least that was totally true. "And I don't know when I'll be out of there, and you have your plans. Why don't we just not see each other on Friday? We'll do Saturday night instead, okay?"

He nodded so easily, it sent a stab of fresh guilt through her. "That's fine," he said. "Hate to admit it, but it might be best. I always get roped into some kind of after-hang with some of the guys, and I have to go along to show face, you know?"

"Sure."

"Tell you what. On Saturday, bring a bag with you. You're coming home with me and staying until Monday morning. Deal?"

She gave a little smile, hoping it didn't look as forced as it felt. "Deal."

He pressed his lips to hers, kissing her tenderly, lingering as his tongue slipped inside to dance with hers. "Tonight was great. Thanks for remembering it was Hanukkah and for thinking of me. Bringing me to the menorah lighting, dinner at the Plaza, all of it. It was fun." He smiled, almost sheepish.

"It was so much more special because you were there with me, Anna. Thanks."

Her nervous insides melted, morphing into goo. The sweet look on his face... She truly adored him. "Aww. You're welcome." Everything will be fine, she thought, demanding it of herself. She kissed him, caressed his face, and whispered, "Happy Hanukkah, handsome."

Chapter Fourteen

D AVID COULD HEAR the thump of the music as soon as he entered the hallway; by the time he got to the wide doors of the ballroom, he could feel the bass vibrating through the soles of his feet. The Taylor Swift version of "Last Christmas" played at top volume. David frowned on the inside; he'd always preferred the original. He straightened his blue patterned silk tie and made sure his black Armani suit jacket was buttoned before entering the room.

The overhead lights weren't on, but a zillion tiny white lights strung around the room and hanging from the ceiling gave more than enough illumination. It was impressive and magical at the same time. Silver bows and red ribbons were all around, giving the room a holiday feel. Over three hundred employees of The Linderton Group filled the large space, talking and drinking and dressed to the nines, as waiters made their way around with silver trays of food and carefully balanced glasses.

David sighed. This was going to be a drag. He'd never been a big party guy, but he also didn't mind them. Usually, big parties filled with schmoozers didn't faze him, and if he drank just enough but not too much, things were fine. But nowadays, he would rather be home watching Netflix or reading, or at a smaller, quieter bar with a few good people.

Ah, who was he kidding? He would rather be at O'Reilly's, nursing a drink with Mike or another friend while he watched Anna from across the room, counting down the minutes until she was done with work. Until he could take her home, strip off her clothes, and have her all to himself in the quiet darkness of his apartment.

He missed her tonight.

Would she be comfortable here, at his company party, if they'd been allowed to bring dates? He figured sure, why not—even though it wasn't her scene, it probably wouldn't faze her, as she didn't seem to ever care what anyone thought of her. So she'd suffer through it for him, say dirty things to make him burn and salty things to make him laugh, and be the most gorgeous, sexiest woman in the whole damn room.

Or… would her tattoos and multi-colored locks drawn raised eyebrows and behind-the-hand snickers from his colleagues' snooty spouses?

The thought made him uncomfortable; both for his thinking it, and for knowing the likely answer deep down.

He let out a sigh. It was speculation. It didn't matter. What mattered was Anna wasn't there, the throbbing Christmas music was too loud, and he didn't feel like working the room. It was going to be a long night.

"Hey, there he is!" Joe, Seth, and Brian approached him.

At least the work friends he liked the most were there. That was something. He shook hands, gave and got slaps on the back, all the male ritual greetings. They talked for a few minutes, shouting to be heard over the music. A waiter floated by with a silver tray of filled champagne flutes, but they declined.

"I need a real drink," Brian said, though he looked like he'd already had a few.

"To the bar!" Joe cried.

"To the bar!" they all echoed, and made their way through the crowd to the far side of the room.

As was now his habit, David's eyes scanned the long bar for the bartenders. It was lit with neon, glass and chrome. So different from O'Reilly's. There were two men and two women tending bar tonight, all of them dressed in black and wearing Santa hats. Two guys, one in his twenties, one in his thirties, both with bushy hipster beards. One woman, tall and skinny, had a long, sleek black ponytail under her Santa hat that went halfway down her back. The other woman down at the far end was... David blinked. No. His eyes were playing tricks on him. He couldn't believe what he was looking at.

The other female bartender was Anna.

His insides seized. She had to have known she was working his company's party. She knew who he worked for. She must have known for at least a few weeks, he'd bet.

His mind went back to their chat in bed about the party.

There had been all the opportunity in the world for her to say, "Hey, guess what? I'll be working that party."

His skin felt too tight and too hot. Why hadn't she said anything? What the hell?

"You didn't even hear me, did you?" Seth shouted in his ear.

"What?" David stammered. "No, um. No. What'd you say?"

"Both of those chicks are hot." Seth's eyes coolly appraised the brunette and Anna. "Don't you think?"

David clamped his mouth shut and just gave a short nod. Joe and Brian were both married, but Seth was still single and probably always would be. He went through women like David went through coffee. When David first met him, a decade before, he'd thought Seth's skills with women were impressive; it seemed there wasn't a woman Seth couldn't seduce. Now, years later, it had grown stale for David, even off-putting. By their age, it wasn't something to be proud of; it was kind of sleazy.

And he sure as hell didn't like the way Seth was looking at his girlfriend.

He swallowed back his annoyance and said, "Haven't you dated most of the women in the city already, bro?"

"There's always a few I haven't met yet," Seth said with a wink.

"So now you're hitting on bartenders at company functions?" David asked, trying to deter him. The words felt like lead in his mouth.

"Not yet. Just looking. I mean, the merchandise is on display, so." He shoved forward to get the brunette's attention.

David's chest burned and his blood raced. He stared down the length of the bar, unwilling to confront Anna directly in front of all his colleagues and superiors. He didn't want to embarrass her, or draw unnecessary attention to himself. But goddammit, he felt blindsided. He just stared at her harder, willing her to feel his stare and make eye contact.

"You okay, man?" Joe asked him. "You look pissed off or something."

"Just too many people at the bar," David ground out.

Brian nodded in agreement. "Who do we have to do to get a drink?"

"Seth's got it," Joe said, watching their friend talk to the brunette.

David kept watching Anna, unable to take his eyes off her. Damn if that Santa hat didn't make her look utterly adorable. It was a little strange to see her behind a bar that wasn't O'Reilly's. She was working as she always did, quickly and efficiently, her eyes on her busy hands but that sunny smile never leaving her face.

This stung. Clearly she hadn't wanted him to know she'd be working his party. Why? Because, independent spirit that she was, she simply didn't want to tell him? Or something more negative? He could feel his heartbeat rising in speed, his blood rushing through his veins. Goddammit, there'd better be a good reason she'd kept this from him. They were going to talk. And she was going to tell him.

Seth handed him a shot glass with clear liquid in it.

"What is this?" David asked.

"Tito's. To start with." He tapped his glass around to all of theirs. "Merry Christmas, gentlemen." They all drank. "Oh, sorry, Happy Hanukkah, Dave."

David knocked back his shot, feeling the vodka burn a trail down his throat and sear through his limbs. "Back in a few." He turned away from his friends and pushed his way through the crowded room until he got to the far end of the long bar. He planted himself right in front of Anna.

She turned to him and he watched her eyes widen a drop. Then she recomposed herself with record speed, flashing him one of her dazzling smiles as she slapped a napkin down on the bar. "Evening. What can I getcha?"

"An explanation," he growled.

She glanced at the people very close, all around him. "Sure you want to do this here?"

His jaw clenched. "No, I don't. But we need to talk. Can you get away for a few minutes?"

"I'm working," she said firmly.

"I see that. An interesting surprise."

Her eyes darted to the left of him; Jim Steadman stood there, watching their exchange. "You getting a drink?" he asked David. "Or can I order?"

"What can I get you, sir?" Anna asked Jim.

"Scotch on the rocks."

"Coming right up." She looked back to David. "And you, sir?"

David's chest ached. This was… he didn't know what it was, but it sucked. "Vodka. Twist of lime. Please."

She arched a brow, knowing that wasn't his usual drink. But that was the only hint he could see. Otherwise, she was acting like she didn't know him.

"Looks like we've got a full house here," Jim said, surveying the crowd as he made small talk.

"Yup," David said.

"Can't believe another year's flown by," Jim said.

"Yup," David said. He didn't want to be shooting the shit with Jim, he wanted to be alone with Anna to get answers, to get a reaction, to get something.

She turned back to them, a glass in each hand, and set them down on the bar. Another dazzling smile appeared as she said, "Enjoy your night, gentlemen."

Jim thanked her and moved away. David stood there as if rooted into the ground. "You don't know me?" He had to shout to be heard above the pounding music. He also felt like shouting. "Is that what we're doing? Is that what we're playing right now?"

Again, she looked at his colleagues, packed in all around him, then back to him with lifted brows and a pointed gaze, as if to say, "Do you see all these people you work with standing here?"

He leaned in close so she could hear him. "Why didn't you tell me you were working this tonight? Why wouldn't you just tell me?"

"I didn't know how'd you take it," she said, not flinching as their eyes locked.

"Why would I take it as anything?" he asked. "You have a job. Okay. You said you work private parties sometimes. But why wouldn't you tell me? I just don't get *why*, Anna. Make me understand, because I want to."

Her heated gaze seared into his. "You really want all these stuck-up people, the people you work with, to know that the bartender at their event, that *I*—" she gestured over herself "—am your girlfriend?" Her blue eyes glittered with challenge. "Somehow, I doubt it. And I didn't feel like putting that to the test."

His mouth fell open. Ten different responses ricocheted through his mind. But what came out was, "Don't tell me what I think."

"Miss?" The gruff voice at his side was Paul Natser, one of the senior managers. He didn't even look at David, only at Anna. "Jim Beam, neat."

"Yes, sir." She smiled at the older man and turned away to make the drink.

David stood and fumed, his mind spinning. She didn't think, didn't trust, that he would have been proud to let people know she was his girlfriend. Damn, damn, dammit to hell. It both hurt him and angered him at the same time.

She thought he'd be ashamed of her.

And then, finally, a lick of shame washed over him. Because the reality was… no, this wasn't the way he would have liked to introduce her to his friends and colleagues. He knew how it'd look. She had too. It would be awkward as hell and possibly embarrassing for both of them.

His face burned with the realization that if he could think those horrible thoughts that she hadn't been wrong about him after all.

When she brought back the drink for Natser, the bastard didn't even thank her, just took his drink and walked away. Another hit that hammered into David. It was men like Natser who made Anna think David would be ashamed to admit he was dating her. Dammit, they needed to talk. "Take a break, Anna. Give me five minutes."

"I can't," she said. "I don't get a break until nine-thirty. So go enjoy the party."

"Are you fucking kidding me?" He wanted to throw something. "Why are you acting like this?"

"Heeeey, man!" Joe, Seth, and Brian were behind him, around him. All three of them were already half drunk. "There you are, brother!"

"Any of you need anything?" Anna asked.

"Oh I need something, all right…" Seth let his words trail off as his dark eyes trailed over her body. He licked his lips.

Fiery rage swept through David in a heartbeat.

But the smile never left Anna's face; only her voice hardened. "Something to *drink*?"

David got in Seth's face and growled at him, "Knock it off. Don't be gross."

"What, man?" Seth laughed. "Chill out. Just checking out what's on display."

"She's not a 'what' and she's not on display," David said, feeling his blood pressure rise. "Just don't."

"Let's do more shots," Brian said.

"I'm already half trashed." Seth laughed, backing away from David.

"You guys should know better," David said. "You don't get shitfaced at a work party. C'mon."

"No one cares," Joe said. "As long as you don't puke on the boss's shoes or do something stupid. Everyone here's half in the bag already."

Seth kept staring at Anna over David's shoulder, giving her a leering grin and a wink.

David gave him a tiny shove back, barely repressing the urge to punch him. "Just leave her alone, okay?"

Seth's brows shot up. "Ohhhhh. You were here before me. I get it. Go for it, bro, she's totally hot."

David cringed inside but only said, "C'mon, let's move. You guys need to eat something."

"That sounds good," Brian said.

David looked back over his shoulder. Anna was already

fixing a drink for someone else. Her cheeks were flushed and she didn't look at him again. He shook his head in disbelief at how this had gone, but didn't want to cause a scene. He dragged his friends away, determined to talk to her later.

The evening was interminable. David could barely pull off making small talk with colleagues, and had had to distance himself from his drunken friends, who were acting like idiots. The music was too damn loud and everyone was annoying him. He just wanted to leave, but of course couldn't until he'd spoken to Anna. So he waited as the minutes dragged by.

He felt like a stalker, watching her all night from various points across the room. He turned her words over and over in his head. They'd come down on him like sledgehammers. The realizations that she thought he'd be ashamed of being seen with her, along with the fact that yes, confronted with the reality of the people in his world and her at the same time, he saw the problem... It all made him feel a little sick.

By nine twenty-five, the party had shifted into a different gear. The over-forty crowd were starting to say their good-byes or had already slipped out; the younger tier was fully loaded and ready to go the distance. David had heard the sniffing in the restroom and knew that if some of these people were coked up, they'd go all night. He'd made the mandatory appearance, made the mandatory small talk with his boss and other managers. He was climbing out of his skin. So at nine twenty-five, he went to the bar and again planted himself directly in front of Anna.

She glanced at him as she finished filling a glass of red wine, but not again as she slid the glass to the woman at his right. The woman thanked her and walked away with her drink.

"What can I get you?" she asked him.

"You get a break in five minutes, right?" he said.

She took her phone from her back pocket, looked at it, and nodded as she put it away. "I get fifteen minutes. I plan to wolf down a sandwich and pee. Not in that order."

"I'm going with you."

"Not a good idea. Also, I didn't invite you along."

He leaned in and hissed, "Why are you doing this?"

Her eyes narrowed as she hissed back, "Because I don't want to have this conversation *here*. Do you?"

"Yes. Yes, I do."

"David. How nice to see you," said a female voice to his left.

Oh God, no. Great, just fucking great. He turned slowly to face his boss's haughty wife. No one was allowed to bring a spouse or significant other, but the CEO's wife came every year. David had managed to avoid face time with Diane McConnell all evening, but it seemed his luck had just run out. "Hello, Diane."

She leaned in and gave him an air kiss, wobbling the slightest bit. She must have already had a few drinks, like most others at the party. Why did he have such rampant animosity toward everyone in his sphere tonight?

"You're looking well," she said.

"Thank you. You look lovely tonight." He hated fawning, though it was a necessary evil, and he kept it to a minimum. Her Botox must have been stellar this round; her face barely moved. She was fashionable as always in a red and black gown that showcased her figure, still fantastic for a woman in her mid-fifties. He wondered fleetingly if the rumors about her affair with her tennis coach were true. She certainly looked fit. "Happy holidays to you."

"And to you." Her nasal drawl was like nails on a chalkboard to him. He braced himself for what he knew would likely be coming. "So, David. Are you seeing anyone these days?"

And there it was. And right in front of Anna. Fanfucking-tastic.

Back in the spring, Diane had tried to set David up with her niece, Courtney. They'd gone on one date. It had been awful. Yes, Courtney was beautiful. She was also too young for him, disgustingly entitled, and obnoxious. But he had to tread carefully. This was Jeremy's wife he was talking to, and his boss's wife was a known tyrant. "Actually," David said, "I am." He glanced at Anna for a second. She was right there, watching and listening. He wished he could explain to her what was happening.

Diane scowled, not bothering to hide her disdain. "Courtney was disappointed you didn't call her again. I can't imagine why you wouldn't. She's a beautiful girl."

"So is the one I'm dating now," David said.

Anna snorted audibly.

Diane huffed out a breath in disgust, sneering. Then she turned to Anna and demanded, "I'll have a Chardonnay."

"Sure," Anna said, placing a napkin on the bar. "Any particular kind?"

"Whatever is oaked, and good." Diane looked down her nose at Anna. "Do you know what's good from what isn't? With ridiculous hair like that, I'm not so sure."

David wanted to kick this woman. But he knew Anna could handle herself.

Anna only smiled. "I believe I do, but if you have a preference, why don't you just tell me exactly what you'd like."

"What I want is a goddamn glass of wine." Diane leaned on the bar. "You need me to spell it out for you? Fine." She glared at Anna. "C-h-a-r-d-o-n-n-a-y."

David gaped openly. The blatant, open rudeness took him totally off guard.

Diane waved a dismissive hand in Anna's direction. "Go on."

Anna just smiled again. "Actually, my break just started. But you can find one of the other bartenders to be a disgusting witch to, I'm sure." She cocked her head to the side as she met Diane's glare with a steely one of her own, but the smile never left her face. "You know, all this time, I thought shallow, Botoxed, empty-headed trophy wives didn't need to know how to spell. You should be so proud of yourself, sweetie." She didn't spare either of them another glance as she walked away.

David watched her go, both impressed with her moxie and desperate to go after her and somehow make things right.

"I need to go find out that little bitch's name so I can have her fired," Diane said.

He swiveled back to the tyrant. "Don't do that. C'mon, where's your holiday spirit?"

"But she—"

"—asked you if you wanted a drink, and you insulted her. So just let it go."

"You let Courtney go," Diane said, and swayed slightly. "You broke her heart."

"We went on one date," he said. "So I highly doubt that." He had to get to Anna. "I'm sorry, will you excuse me?"

Diane started to protest, but he practically ran away from her. He shoved through the sea of his fellow bankers to the other end of the bar, where the older of the two male bartenders was. "Excuse me. Could you tell me where Anna went?"

The bearded guy, tall and muscular, eyed him warily. "She went on her break."

"I need to talk to her," David said.

"Are you the one who just pissed her off?" the bearded

guy asked. His gaze could turn someone to stone.

"No," David said, although he had a feeling that wasn't totally true. "I'm her boyfriend. I need to find her. Please."

"Hold on." The guy pulled his phone out of his pocket and thumbed in a text. "What's your name?"

"David. She knows I'm here."

The bearded man stared down at his phone as he waited, not looking up at David. The minute felt like a month to him. He knew he should be grateful that this guy clearly had Anna's back, protecting her if David wasn't who he said he was. But he was getting more and more tense by the second.

Finally, Beardo looked up and said, "No dice, man. Sorry." He held up the phone so David could see the screen.

Vince: *Guy here looking 4 u. Says he's ur boyfriend, David. Is he?*

Anna: *yes*

Vince: *Says he needs to see u. Okay to send him back?*

Anna: *NO. Tell him no. Thx*

David felt his stomach clench. Clearly, Anna wasn't going to give him an inch as long as they were at this stupid party. He'd have to get to her another way, another time. "Fine. Thanks." He turned away, stormed through the crowd, and left the party.

Chapter Fifteen

ANNA YAWNED AGAIN. She was so tired, the rocking of the subway car was actually sending her to sleep. She fought to keep her eyes open. All she wanted was to get home, get into her bed, and sleep for a week.

Maybe if she slept that long, she wouldn't think about David.

She'd known not cluing him into the fact that she'd be working his company's holiday party might be a mistake, but she just hadn't had the guts to tell him. She'd told herself it was because if he'd shown any dismay beforehand, she might not have been able to work the party.

But now, after thinking of nothing else all night, she knew that wasn't *all* of the truth. The truth was darker, uglier. The truth was, she'd assumed he'd be embarrassed to see her there. Embarrassed to possibly have to introduce her to his colleagues as his new girlfriend as she worked behind the bar. That he'd see her in his environment, surrounded by his people... and finally realize that no, she wasn't good enough for him, and she didn't fit into his life after all.

So she'd made a mess of it. Pure self-sabotage. A classic

Anna move.

She couldn't stop thinking of the look in his eyes; it haunted her. The mixture of emotions there: disbelief, anger, confusion, and worst of all, the hurt. She hadn't meant to hurt him. He was usually so cool, calm, and collected. She'd never seen his temper flare like that before. The heated frustration he'd shown and his biting words had only underscored how hurt he clearly was.

The thing was, he'd stung her in return, and likely without him even realizing that he had. And that stuck in her throat like a lump she couldn't swallow down.

But yes, this was mostly on her, and she knew she owed him an explanation. If she could only explain it better to herself, that would be helpful too.

The train lurched, shifting her hard in her seat and jolting her. It was like the universe giving her a shove and telling her to get herself together. She sighed, closed her eyes, and leaned her head back against the wall of the subway car. She was a skilled self-saboteur, but she had honor. She would call him in the morning, ask if they could have lunch and talk. Getting it over with before she went to work on Saturday evening seemed the best thing to do. Drawing it out wasn't fair to him, or good for her.

Now if she could figure out how to say what she wanted, needed, to say… it all jumbled around in her brain like marbles. Good Lord, she just wanted her bed.

At her stop, she grabbed her messenger bag and slung the

wide strap over her shoulder, cross-body style as she exited the train. She pushed the Santa hat more securely onto her head; that was a fun souvenir she'd use at O'Reilly's, since she'd lost the one she had last year. A fresh surge of antsy unease shot through her. She walked quickly through the station, shoved through the turnstile, then raced up the stairs to get to the street.

The cold night air whipped her face and sent the ends of her hair dancing around her shoulders. She found her gloves in her coat pockets and pulled them on as she walked, eager to just get home. Her building was only four blocks from the subway station. The frigid air and the buzz in her blood threatened to give her a second wind. She hoped not, since it was one-thirty in the morning. If she got a second wind now, she wouldn't be able to fall asleep 'til daybreak. That had happened too many times before, and she always paid for it at work the next night.

But when she turned the corner, she only took a few steps before stopping short. A man was sitting on the concrete steps in front of her building. Blue ski jacket, jeans, sneakers, and skullcap hat, his elbows on his knees as he stared down at his phone. The light from the small screen illuminated his face, and she sucked in a breath. "David?"

His head lifted and his eyes met hers. "I hoped you'd get home soon. I'm freezing and dead tired."

"So am I." Her blood buzzed in her veins, carrying adrenaline to the ends of her limbs and lighting up every nerve. Her bones felt liquidy. "It's so late. Please tell me you haven't been waiting here all this time."

"Not the whole time, no. About half an hour." He rose to stand, shoving his phone into his jeans pocket. White puffs left his mouth as he spoke. "After your bearded friend showed me your emphatic 'no' text, I left the party."

"I thought so," she said. "Since I didn't see you again. I figured you were either staying away from me, or you'd left altogether."

"I couldn't stand being there another minute." He stuffed his hands into the pockets of his ski jacket as he stared at her. "I went home. Sat there fuming, thinking, trying to figure out what the hell… Dammit, Anna, why wouldn't you just tell me you were working the party?" A muscle jumped in his jaw. "I'm not going to touch you, but I'm not leaving until you've told me. You can't put me off now, it's just you and me. No bar between us, no people around us, no reason not to talk." His gaze was unflinching as he added, "You want to step around me and go inside, blow me off, fine. But if you do, you won't hear from me again. I don't like games like this."

Her heart rate skyrocketed. It was kind of amazing, how he stayed and sounded calm, but was clearly frustrated and furious. It radiated off him in waves. And he was throwing it down. The blaze in his eyes was lethal.

"I'm not playing games," she said quietly. "And I'm not going to blow you off." She tried to take a deep breath.

"You're right, we do need to talk. I'm just exhausted. It's been a long night."

"Tell me about it."

The wind blew harshly, whipping both of them until their eyes teared. "Do you want to come upstairs?" she finally asked. "To talk?"

"Yes," he said.

Anna could almost feel her heartbeat pulsing in her fingertips. "I'm sure Billy is sleeping," she said quietly as she unlocked her door. "So let's try to keep it down, okay?"

David nodded and followed her inside.

The overhead lights were off but the Christmas tree lights were on. Usually, the sight was one that made Anna smile with childlike happiness. But not tonight She flipped the overheads on and exhaled when she spotted the red lace thong on the end table next to the remote. "He's not here. He's out. It's okay, we don't have to whisper."

"What do you mean?" David asked, standing stiffly by the door.

She scooped up the scrap of lace and held it out to him before shoving it into the small drawer of the end table. "This is what we use to tell each other that we went out for the night and not to worry."

David frowned, shot her a sideways look. "You leave a red pair of panties on the table as your sign? Interesting choice." One brow arched. "You can't write a note?"

"It's a long story," she said, shrugging out of her silver

coat. "It's actually a funny story, but I'm not going to tell it now." She reached up and pulled the Santa hat off her head. She had a feeling this discussion wasn't going to be festive, and she couldn't take herself seriously with the hat on, much less expect him to. "Take off your coat, stay a while."

He hesitated, then unzipped the jacket and pulled off his hat, dropping both onto the end of the couch. They stood across the small room, staring at each other. Tension radiated and crackled between them like electric currents.

"Just tell me," David said. "Explain tonight, please. I can't figure you out."

Anna sighed and sat on the couch, motioning him to join her. He sat on the other end, putting as much distance between them as possible. The move pierced her heart. He usually couldn't get close enough or keep his hands off her. "David…"

"You knew it was my company when you were offered the job," he said. "You know damn well who I work for. So don't tell me you didn't know."

"I won't. Of course I knew. I knew immediately, like you said."

"Okay. So…" Eyes wide, he threw up his hands in a gesture of pure frustration.

"I think I was protecting myself," she said softly. She should tell him all of it, right then. Tell him how she was afraid he'd leave her. Tell him about Christopher, tell him how what he'd said and done had screwed with her head in ten different ways. But she couldn't. So she went with most of the truth, not all of it. "I didn't want to hear you be… disparaging. Condescending. Make a bad joke about it. Tell me I shouldn't work the party because you didn't want to see me there. Or worse, say something to make me feel less than you. Because if you did, it would've broken my heart."

He leaned in, brows furrowed as he peered into her eyes. "What have I ever done to even put those thoughts in your head?"

She swallowed hard, held in place by his gaze. *Tell him. Tell him what happened. Maybe then he'll understand.*

"Have I ever, *ever*, treated you with anything but respect?" he asked, pain and confusion lacing his words.

"No," she whispered. "But… we've been kind of a secret, haven't we? In our own little bubble. I haven't met your friends, you've barely met mine. We've had this wonderful, exciting, delicious secret thing together. Maybe that's most of the appeal for you. It being a hidden thing. But we've never… exposed it to the light, you know? Our worlds are so different… maybe too different. I don't know that we'll fit into each other's lives, David. And I… I didn't want to hear you say the same thing."

He kept staring at her, that intense gaze searing into her bones. "You thought if I saw you working behind the bar at my party, I'd be ashamed. Or ignore you, or possibly something worse. Is that right?"

Her cheeks flamed at the harshness of his words as she

nodded.

"That's not fair, Anna," he said in a low tone. "Not only did I think you were savvier than that, but it's also just wrong."

"Is it?" Her mouth felt dry, but she had to say it. "That bitch on wheels insulted me to my face, and you didn't tell her to shut her mouth."

"First of all, I was just stunned speechless. I really was. I couldn't believe she did that. Second, I know you're a badass. You didn't need me to take Diane down for you—you can do that yourself. And you did, before I could even formulate something coherent to say." His lips twitched with a hint of a grin. "You were awesome, actually."

"You don't get it." She sighed. "Yes, I'm capable of taking care of myself. But it would have been nice if you said something to stand up for me, just because it would've been the right thing to do. Whether it was for me, or any woman. You know? And you didn't. That sucked."

David sighed. "Okay. I get that. I see your point. I'm sorry."

"Okay, great, but that wasn't even your first offense of the night." Anna felt adrenaline sear through her body as her anger reheated. "How come you didn't say anything to your asshole friend when he was looking me over like I was a piece of meat?"

David's head cocked as he frowned. "What?"

"You know what I'm talking about."

"You mean Seth? He was drunk, and he *is* an asshole. Don't mind him."

Anna felt her face heat, felt the burn down into her chest as her heart rate rose. "When he leered at me, yeah it was repulsive. And that time, you didn't think, 'Anna can handle herself'; yes, you told him to back off. But you *didn't* say, 'Back off because that's my girlfriend you're hitting on'." She licked her suddenly dry lips. "Because you didn't want your co-workers and friends to know you're dating the bartender."

"Anna, no. That's not…"

"That's not true? Don't lie to me."

"Maybe it was a little bit true, but not for the reasons you think."

"Do you think I'm stupid?"

"No!" He raked his hands through his hair. "That's not what it was about. I didn't want him looking at you or talking to you like that, so I just wanted to get him to stop as fast as possible."

"Yes, but—"

"And I *did*. I got him to leave you alone."

"Okay, you stood up for a woman, yes. Hooray for you. But you didn't stand up for *your* woman. Did you?" Her jaw set tighter as she stared right back. "Did you? Nope. And I got that loud and clear."

He swore under his breath. "You're making this into something it wasn't."

"No, I'm not. Do you even get what you did?" Anna

didn't want to yell, but her voice was definitely getting louder. "First him, then the Botox Queen. You said you were dating someone. *Someone.* I was standing right fucking there!"

"I know."

"You didn't say, 'And hey, look, here she is!' And you didn't say, 'Don't talk to my girlfriend that way.' Right?"

"I didn't want her aiming her toxicity at you," he said miserably.

"She did anyway."

"I didn't want more of it aimed your way."

"You're lying to me, and to yourself," Anna insisted. "Because it was just like I thought it might be—you didn't want to admit you knew me in front of the people in your orbit. That's the truth."

"Goddammit!" He jumped up from the couch and started pacing the small room, eating up the tiny space between the walls. "You're not innocent here. You purposely lied to me."

"I didn't lie to you."

"No, but you kept the truth from me. Purposeful omission. It's the same damn thing, Anna."

She didn't say anything to that, but she nodded.

"Okay! You finally admit something." His pacing reminded her of a caged tiger: lean, lethal, fierce, and radiating carnal power. "Now. How about we address the fact that on top of your lie of omission, when I *did* get there, you acted like you didn't know me! So for you to put this all on me, that's not fair."

"Don't talk to me about fair," she spat.

"How about I talk to you about the truth, then? The truth is, you speculated and made assumptions, then made my choice for me."

"You want to talk about the truth?" she cried. "You were ashamed to tell your friends or that viper that I'm your woman. *That's* the truth. It's all over your face."

"With Seth, I didn't want to make a scene," he said. "I just wanted to defuse the situation as quickly as possible, get him away from you." His cheeks were flushed, his eyes flashed; David looked ready to explode. "Seth is a skank. He's slept with half the women in the city. I didn't want him to even look at you, much less talk to you."

"Nice friends ya got there," she remarked.

"He's a work friend, not a real friend. We started at the same time."

"I really don't care, actually."

"Fine. Great."

"And the Botox Queen? Who's Courtney?"

David groaned. "The Botox Queen is my boss's wife. She's hell on earth. Courtney is her niece. They set us up on a blind date a few months ago, and that was hell on earth too. This girl was twenty-three—way too young for me— and the kind of spoiled princess you think all rich women are. I couldn't get away from her fast enough that night, and

I never called her or led her on, none of that."

"All the people you know are so charming," Anna remarked dryly.

"No, they're not all like that," he growled. "But I didn't... I wasn't pretending I didn't know you. It wasn't like you said."

She got to her feet and stopped him from pacing with a hand on his chest. "You didn't say I was your girlfriend. You didn't even say you knew me. You could have."

"You were the one who was acting like you didn't even know me first."

"David. Stop deflecting."

"Okay. Fine. Fine!" He raked his hands through his hair. "No, that wasn't the ideal way to introduce you to those people."

She took a step back, her blood turning cold. "Uh huh."

"But you also have to stop projecting."

"Maybe."

"Not maybe. Yes, I didn't tell anyone tonight we're dating. But you didn't need me to be your knight in shining armor. You never do. You have your own sword."

That made her pulse kick up. "Let me tell you something," she said, seething. "I was hit on right in front of you. If some skank, as you said, was hitting on you in front of me? I'd've gotten in her face and set her straight in a heartbeat. And if some super nasty person insulted you in front of me? Even though I *know* you can handle yourself, I'd've said something, simply because it's the right thing to do." She didn't blink as they stared each other down. "You didn't do *any* of that for me."

His jaw set as his face paled.

"You didn't want to make a scene," Anna said, her heart pounding. "Your own words, just now. So I speculated, but guess what? I was right. Your actions tonight told me I'm not worth making a scene. I got that loud and clear."

She saw the look on his face change as realization set in. His eyes rounded, and he looked ashen. He licked his lips and stammered, "I'm sorry, Anna. I'm sorry."

"Okay. You finally get it. Thanks."

"You're absolutely right. I'm so sorry."

"I know I'm right." She saw the remorse in his eyes, but only felt sick to her stomach. "Why didn't I tell you I'd be there in the first place? Because I didn't want to deal with you having to pretend you didn't know me in front of your peers. Which is exactly what happened. Right?"

"No." He grasped her shoulders. "I mean… yes, I should have said that, and done that, everything you said. You're absolutely right. But I was off my game, because I wasn't expecting you to be there, much less you were treating me like a stranger and I couldn't understand it."

"Oh. I see. So it's *my* fault you didn't think to stand up for me." She shook off his hands.

"No, no, that's not what I meant." Again he raked his hands through his hair as his eyes flashed. He reached for her but she stepped back. He swore vehemently under his breath. "Yes, I should have stood up for you. I should have come to your defense as your boyfriend, and I didn't, and that's on me. But like I said, I guess I thought you really didn't need me to, Anna. You're a strong, kickass woman. You don't need me to be your defender."

She sighed and started to say something, but he added, "Plus, you struck first. You didn't trust me enough to tell me you were working the party. That part is on you. And you're just avoiding that completely. It's easier to blame all this on me. You deliberately kept something from me. How I acted was wrong, yes. But where's your part? I'm not hearing it."

That made her freeze. She nodded slowly, her heart pounding and her stomach a nauseous whirl. She couldn't do this. She didn't want to do this. Summoning stillness, she drew a deep breath and sat back down on the couch. She looked up at him. Christ, he was so beautiful. It hurt to look at him. "You need to leave now. Close the door on your way out."

He blinked a few times, gaping at her. His hands flexed a few times before he shoved them in his pockets. "So you're dismissing me? And that's it?"

"Yes," she said quietly, misery and nausea flooding her entire system. "I think we're done here."

He stared at her for a few seconds longer, then grabbed his coat and yanked it on. "You know what's interesting, Anna? I did hear you. I did apologize. I did see that you had valid points. Yes, I realize I screwed up. And I mean it. But I still haven't heard a word from you that you're sorry for what you did too." He zipped up his coat and pushed his hat onto his head, eyes blazing. "It's all on me? I'm the bad guy, and now we're through? That's how you're going to spin this? Okay." He headed for the door and slammed it hard behind him.

Anna sat very still, staring at the door for a long time. A few tears rolled down her cheeks, and she numbly wiped them away.

Chapter Sixteen

S UNDAY MORNINGS WEREN'T the same without her.

David lay in bed, his hands laced behind his head. For a long while, he watched the patterns the dappled sunlight made on the ceiling and the walls. He'd barely slept since Friday night. He'd spent Saturday in an angry, sad daze as he ran his errands and went through the motions, flipping Anna's words and the events over and over in his head. Last night, he'd stayed in and gotten work done. He worked past midnight, hoping against hope that she would come see him after she got off work, like she sometimes did. Hoping she'd appear so they could talk, work things out… By three A.M., he knew that wasn't happening, and drifted off in misery.

In a very short time, he'd gotten used to having Anna McKinnon in his life. And her sudden absence felt like a big, black hole.

He was in love with her. Yes, it'd only been seven weeks since they'd met. But that was the only reason it could hurt this much to have lost her.

He picked up his phone from the nightstand. No texts from her. Nothing since she'd told him to leave on Friday night.

She'd been right, of course. That killed him. She'd been absolutely fucking dead-on when she pointed out he hadn't stood up for her the right way. God, he was stupid. He always considered himself to be something of a gentleman, and he'd been a wimp. A thoughtless, cowardly jerk. He had indeed proven her fears right, in more ways than one.

But not all the ways. Something still didn't add up, didn't make sense. She'd been wrong too, and she refused to own her part. Yet he wasn't willing to let it go. Or let *her* go. He needed to grovel a little, and then convince her to give them another shot. Because the thought of not having her in his life was simply unacceptable.

Especially with only a little more than a week to Christmas. He was not going to lose her, or let her be mad at him, or worst of all, let her be hurt so close to Christmas when she loved the holiday so much. That was also unacceptable.

With new determination, he threw back the covers. *Operation Get Her Back, starting now.* He got out of bed and went to the kitchen to make coffee. While he did, he sent her texts. It was only ten, and he knew she'd probably be asleep until noon, but he had to try, and he had to start trying right then.

> **David:** All I've done since I left your apartment is think about you.

> **David:** I miss you like hell, Anna. It hurts to have lost you. I'm hurting. And I know I hurt you too, and I'm so sorry for

that.

David: *You were right, I screwed up. I should've said you were my girlfriend. I should have shouted it in their damn faces. I was wrong.*

David: *But if you give me another chance, I promise you that will never happen again.*

David: *I am proud to be with you when we're together. I'm willing to stand up for you. I'm sorry I ever made you doubt it.*

David: *Yes, I didn't want to make a scene at my office holiday party. But I could have defused both situations without making scenes. I'm not proud of myself. I'm owning it.*

David: *But…*

David: *At the same time, you kept something big from me. You should have told me you were working the party.*

David: *I wish I knew why you were so sure I'd snub you. I wish you'd tell me about that. I feel like there's more to the story there than you're telling me.*

David: *Because I've only treated you with respect. I even asked you that last night, to make sure I have, and you said yes.*

David: *Except, of course, at the party. And again, I'm so sorry. You made me see how I messed up. You were right. I am taking responsibility for my part.*

David: *I am groveling, and I should be. This is me groveling, Anna.*

David: *Please consider having dinner with me tonight. Let's talk. Let's work this out.*

David: *We're good together, Anna. We enjoy each other. This is something really special.*

David: *I think you might feel the same way. I hope you do.*

David: *Yes, different worlds and all that. Yes. That's real.*

David: *Yes, seeing you in my 'world' made me see the possible issues you'd talked about.*

David: *Yes, introducing you while you were working the bar wasn't how I wanted to introduce you, both for your sake and for mine. I'm ashamed of that.*

David: *But I'm not ashamed of YOU.*

David: *I don't know how you'll fit into my world some of the time. It might be bumpy. I'm admitting that.*

David: *Maybe you don't want to try. But I want to try.*

David: *Give me the chance to try again.*

David: *I want the chance to work out how we can fit into each other's worlds. You're worth it.*

David: *I care about you. I'm crazy about you. I don't want to lose you.*

David: *Please get back to me when you wake up. I want to work this out.*

David: *I miss you already. You have no idea how much.*

David: *Babe, please answer me. Please.*

ANNA READ THE texts for the fifth time. Most of them had come in while she was still asleep. The last one had come in at three-fifteen, and its openly desperate tone had made her heart squeeze.

She'd barely gotten out of bed all day. She'd slept until one in the afternoon, seen all of David's texts, and had lain there to wallow and think.

Yes, David hadn't stood up for her, and all the things she'd pointed out to him. But he was right: a lie of omission was still a lie. She was wrong too. She had kept something from him, blindsided him with it, and then got mad when all he had time to do was react. That wasn't fair, and she knew it. The residue of shame for her actions trickled through her all day long.

She ate some pretzels and finished a pint of mint chocolate chip ice cream for lunch. In bed. She thought and thought. She cried a little. She grabbed her laptop, curled up under her covers, and watched classic Christmas cartoons on YouTube. The heartsick ache inside didn't lessen in any way.

Finally, a bit before six o'clock, she texted him back. He'd poured his guts out. He'd taken responsibility for his part, all but begged her to see him again and to answer him… His words had moved her.

And the fact was, she had some groveling to do too.

Anna: *hi*

Anna: *I don't know if ur around, but I*

David: *I'm here. Hi*

Anna: *hi*

David: *Please have dinner with me tonight. Or just a drink. Whatever you want.*

David: *But let's meet. Talk in person, not texts, not the phone.*

Anna: *okay*

David: *Fantastic. Tell me where and I'll meet you.*

Anna: *I need to shower. Um…*

David: *Have you eaten dinner yet?*

Anna: *no*

David: *Me neither. Dinner, then?*

Anna: *yes*

David: *Where? Name it.*

Anna: *Meet me at Tratelli's. I want pasta. 7:15?*

David: *Great. See you then.*

WHEN ANNA WALKED into Tratelli's, the heavenly scent of garlic cooking hit her and made her stomach rumble. Decorated for the holidays, strings of multicolored, twinkling lights and fake pine were everywhere, adding a sparkle to the atmosphere. The small Italian restaurant was one of her favorites. She'd only gone there once before with David. But clearly he remembered it, because he was already there. Sitting in a booth near the back, he raised his hand so she'd see him. Her heart skipped a nervous beat and she approached him, her heartbeat pounding in her ears.

"Hi." She shoved her bag into her side of the booth, took off her coat and hat, and quickly ran her fingers through her hair. It was hard to look at him straight on.

But David watched her like a hawk. He didn't move to get up and kiss or hug her hello. He didn't even try to touch her. His hazel eyes drank her in as he said, "You look beautiful."

She gave a tiny snort. She hadn't dressed sexy for him; she just wore a white tunic sweater, leggings with colorful Christmas elves on them, and her red lace-up boots. "Well, thanks." The intensity of his gaze made her slightly uneasy. Usually, she loved basking in it. She liked knowing she had his full and enrapt attention. But now, it only made her feel scrutinized, exposed, and vulnerable.

Before they could say anything more, a waitress appeared with menus. She listed some specials, took their orders, and walked away. As soon as she did, David blurted out, "I'm sorry, Anna. You were right about everything. Everything you pointed out about my behavior on Friday night, the things you said. I'm very sorry, and I'll do better in the future. Not just for you, but for myself."

"Thank you. That's… good to hear. I appreciate it." She finally looked directly at him. Her stomach gave a little flip. Good Lord, he was a bit of a mess. A beautiful mess, but he was clearly as affected by the split as she was. Yes, the black pullover sweater made him look edible, but heavy dark stubble covered his jaw and there were dark circles under his sad eyes. His cool, poised veneer was intact, but those giveaways tipped her off that he was as miserable as she was.

He stared at her, clearly waiting for her to say something.

When she didn't, he murmured, "I want to work things out. I want you in my life. I want to try." His earnest tone and gaze both pierced her heart. "You've come to mean a lot to me in a short time, Anna. I don't want this to be over."

Her body slumped a bit as she stared back. "I don't want it to be over either."

"That's great. That's wonderful. So…" His eyes implored her. "Talk to me."

A lump formed in Anna's throat. She tried to swallow it back, but it felt lodged there. "I'm sorry too. I should have told you I was working the party. It *was* a lie of omission. You had every right to be mad at me."

"Okay." His shoulders relaxed and a hint of a relieved smile played on his full lips. "So can you tell me why you did that? Because that's what I can't figure out. I just don't get *why*. Something else is going on there. It has been all along."

"You're right." She was tired of holding it in. This was too important. She took a deep breath… and the words came pouring out. "Three years ago, I dated this guy Christopher. He came into the bar one night. Instant chemistry. He was drop-dead gorgeous. Funny and charming. And, I found out soon enough, filthy rich. Born and raised on the Upper East Side. A trust fund baby who went to an Ivy League school and now was a hedge fund manager, working in the same firm his father did, and his grandfather before that. One of those big-money family legacies." She looked up at the waitress as she brought the bottle of Rioja to the table and set it down in the center. "Oh thank God." Anna all but grabbed the glass out of her hand. She was going to need a few drinks to get through this conversation.

David poured the wine, filling her glass first, then his. "Go on. You were saying? Christopher?"

"Right…" Anna took a big gulp of wine. The robust taste flamed on her tongue. "I fell fast and hard. The sex was amazing, we had fun together. He was smart, sexy, charismatic. And yes, we were from totally different worlds, so maybe that made it a little more exciting. You starting to get me?"

David nodded, and she knew her Ivy Leaguer was putting two and two together.

So she continued. "But it was about two months before I realized we never went out together in public. It was kind of like it's been with you, because of my hours. I'd meet him at his place after I got off work, we'd have our time together, and I'd go home. But unlike with you, we never spent full days together, never went walking around the city together, nothing. He either came to the bar, or I went to his apartment. He didn't like sleepovers and I didn't push for them. So our nights together… that was it. And after a while, I wanted more. As most people would."

David only nodded as she talked, sipping his wine and listening.

"So, one day, after dating—if you can even really call it dating—for about six months, I finally said, 'Let's go out and do something. Let's go to a museum, a concert, something, anything.' And he looked at me like I had three heads." Anna's lips twisted acerbically, a hollow attempt at a grin. "He told me he didn't want to do that. What if someone he knew saw us together? And he'd have to explain me to them, which he didn't want to do."

David's jaw set and his eyes flashed with indignation. "Seriously?"

"Yeah. I was his regular booty call. That was it." Anna took another gulp from her glass. "He pointed out, in defending himself, that he'd never made me any promises, never said we were exclusive, never talked long term with me. He said, and I quote, 'There are girls that you date and girls that you marry. I can't even date someone like you, much less marry someone like you. I can't bring a *bartender* home to my family. Yeah, we have fun together, but that's all this is. I'm seeing other women too. I thought you knew that.'"

David's face darkened. "That bastard. That disgusting piece of shit." His hands curled into fists on the tabletop.

"Yeah. I remember it word for word, because I was so… blindsided. Then mortified. It made me feel like absolute crap. It made me feel dirty, somehow." She shrugged, took another sip of wine. It was rich and delicious. She considered drinking the whole bottle before she went home. "But also it made me ragey. Like, Hulk-level rage. So, needless to say, we had an ugly fight, said horrible things to each other, and I walked out. Never spoke to him again."

"Good for you."

"Yeah." Another gulp of wine. "He texted for a few weeks, but I didn't answer. He didn't have the balls to actually show up at O'Reilly's ever again. Which is too bad, because if he had, I would've had the pleasure of asking Sean, John, or Jimmy to literally throw his sorry arse out." She shrugged again and looked away.

"But why would he have come back and tried?" she murmured. "I was nothing to him. A low-class piece of arse, a good time, his walk on the wild side. That's all I ever was to him, that fucking snob. *He* was the garbage person, but damn if he didn't make me feel like *I* was. And it hurt like hell. It hurt my heart, my ego, and my pride. So…"

Thinking back on that time made her want to curl up into a ball all over again, but she wouldn't give that jerk the power. She slowly exhaled a deep, cleansing breath as her eyes followed the strings of twinkling lights along the walls. "That's why I've been how I've been with you, David. Okay? It's not right, and I'm sorry. The truth is, I've been waiting for you to pull a Christopher."

"Oh God." David winced and shook his head. "Anna, I'd never—"

"And the thought of seeing you at your office party, surrounded by people who are probably all like Christopher… as in, they see me the way he did, and maybe you would too…" Her eyes stayed glued to her wineglass. "So yes, I assumed. I projected. And that wasn't fair to you. You've been nothing but good to me. I should've told you I was going to be working the party, and I didn't. And to make it worse, I was a bitch to you when we were there. All that's on me. I'm sorry, David. I'm really sorry."

"Okay. Okay." He reached across the table for her hands. "Anna." Slowly, she placed hers in his. The contact from his warm skin sent electric currents up her arms. "Look at me, baby."

She did. The warmth and affection that radiated from him made her heart flutter.

He squeezed her hands gently and spoke in a soft tone. "Knowing what I know now, I get why you were scared to trust me. I wish you'd told me sooner, but I totally understand why you didn't."

"Thanks."

"No, thank *you*, for opening yourself up like this and telling me what happened with him. I can see how much it... I'm so sorry he hurt you that way, sweetheart." He gave her hands another squeeze, caressed her fingers with his. "He was a total asshole, you know that, right?"

"Hell yeah I do. But it hurt then. And... I admit it, it stayed with me."

"Of course it did. It was despicable, how he treated you. Just disgusting. But it was *his* loss. And I'm glad he lost you... because it made you free for me to find you. And I'm very glad I did." He shifted their hands, interlacing their fingers. "I understand the parallels you saw between him and me. I don't like it, but of course I get it."

She simply nodded again. With him being so sweet and thoughtful about it all, it made her feel stupid and childish that she'd held it in for so long. But she was glad he knew, and that she'd owned her part in this mess.

"Now," he said. "Has our affair been a walk on the wild side for me? Yes, in a way. Because I've never dated anyone as free-spirited, colorful, vibrant, and captivating as you. You're a whirlwind. You're fun and brash and full of light. It's been amazing." He continued rubbing her hands between his, gently caressing, strokes of pure affection that went straight to her bruised heart. "I've enjoyed our time together so much, baby."

"Yeah, I'm a good time," she murmured.

"You are. I'm not going to deny that. But my God, Anna, you're so much more than that." His voice sharpened and his gaze intensified, both holding her under his spell. "You're a badass. You don't take crap from anyone. You're independent and smart and resilient. You're funny and sweet and kind. You're creative. I mean… you color your hair to match the seasons. You wear the loudest clothes and you rock them. You love your family so much you tattooed *eleven* butterflies on your spine. You love Christmas like you're still a kid. You never lose your smile through an eight-hour stretch on your feet behind a bar. You're not afraid of hard work. You swear like a sailor. You make me look at things differently. You make me want things I never knew I wanted. You sigh sometimes in your sleep and it's the sweetest sound I've ever heard." His voice softened as he said with reverence, "You're genuinely beautiful inside and out. So unbelievably beautiful."

She blinked in astonishment, stunned speechless.

He raised her hands to his lips and kissed one, then the other. "I'm in love with you, Anna. I want you in my life. I want to make room for you, and I want you to make room for me. I want to introduce you to my family and my friends, and I want to meet yours. I want to take you places, wherever you want to go. It might be bumpy sometimes. But I don't care about what anyone thinks but you. So please give me another chance to show you off to the world, and to treat you like the damn queen that you are. Let's be together. In every way."

Her lips parted, but she couldn't string together a coherent sentence. She blinked at him in wonder.

He grinned. "You look… like you're in shock."

"I am," she finally managed.

"That's a good thing. I think."

"I… Christ, you made me tongue-tied."

"That must be a first. I consider that a high compliment."

She breathed out a laugh. "You really feel that way about me?"

He peered harder into her eyes. "Every word."

"Wow." Her mouth felt dry. She cleared her throat and

licked her lips. "I'm just… I mean… those were the most beautiful things anyone's ever said to me in my whole life. You knocked me flat here."

"Good. I've never gushed at anyone like this before. I meant all of it."

"Thank you. Um… you're in love with me?"

"Yes. Is that okay?"

A stunned giggle flew out of her. "I suppose so."

"Oh good." His smile lit up his whole face.

She wanted to vault the table and climb on him. "I… I feel pretty strongly for you too. But I'm not going to say that I love you until I'm totally sure, David. I don't want to be dishonest in any way."

"That's fine. I respect that. I respect *you*." He let his fingers trail down her cheek, along her jawline. "Yes, there are differences between us. Some people… yeah, they might have something to say. But I don't care."

"You sure about that?"

"I am, yes." He retook her hands in both of his and said, "I know I hurt you the other night, but I've learned from that. Give me another shot and I'll prove it to you. But at the same time… you have to try to trust me more, sweetheart."

"I know," she whispered.

"I hate it, but now I really understand why you were afraid to trust me, trust us, to… hope for more." He squeezed her hands again, rubbed them to assure her. "Honey… I'm not Christopher. If this is going to work, you have to let me in fully if you want us to find middle ground. Can you do that?"

"I can try. Yes." She felt like her heart expanded in her chest. "And I want to try."

"Great." He smiled wide, sparks of relief in his eyes. "So let's make each other happy. Go all in. Okay?"

Her throat felt thick and there was a sting behind her eyes. She wanted to be with him, and to believe in him, more than she'd ever wanted anything in her life.

She took a deep breath, squeezed his hands, and took the leap. "Okay. Yes."

"Thank God." He rose to go around to her side of the booth and slid in beside her. His warm body felt so good next to her. Smiling until the corners of his eyes crinkled, he cradled her face in his hands and kissed her, long and sweet. "I missed you so damn much," he whispered against her lips. "I love you, Anna. We can do this."

"You're wonderful," she whispered back, and kissed him until the waitress arrived with their dinners.

Chapter Seventeen

A NNA STIRRED SLOWLY, pulled from sleep by the sound of the tapping of keys on a keyboard and the scent of strong coffee.

She smiled. The delicious aroma of the gourmet dark roast that David always brewed was now one of her favorite scents. With a yawn, she opened her eyes to see him beside her in bed. He was sitting up, shirtless, hair mussed and unshaven, open laptop on his lap, his intense stare focused on the screen. Christ, he was sweet eye candy. She snuggled closer to him, finding his enticing nakedness under the comforter.

He looked down at her with an affectionate smile. "Good morning." The timbre of his deep voice sent a shimmer of pleasure through her. He ran the backs of his fingers along her cheek. "Sleep well?"

"Yes, once you finally *let* me go to sleep."

"You're insatiable. I was simply doing my duty to make sure you were thoroughly worn out so you could get good sleep."

"Lucky me. Mission accomplished."

He shifted slightly, bending to be able to kiss her. His mouth lingered on hers, savoring, as his hands wandered.

"What time is it?" she asked.

"A bit past eleven."

Her eyes flew wide. "Is—isn't it Monday?"

"It is," he said. "All day."

"But you have work!" Suddenly wide awake, she sat up to face him.

He gestured at the laptop balanced on his legs. "Working from home. I called in. I'm taking today off. Kinda."

"What? Why?" She looked him over. "Are you not feeling well?"

Amusement curved his lips up. "Do I look sick?"

"No. You look gorgeous. But why—"

"Because I wanted to spend the day with you. I thought it was important that we spend today together, after how close we came to being over." He dropped a quick kiss on the tip of her nose, then her mouth. "Today is for us, babe."

Her heart gave a little squeeze. That man lived for his job. He'd taken the day off, a likely busy Monday no less, to be with her? "You're quite the romantic."

"When it comes to you, I just might be. Don't tell anyone. It'll ruin my rep as a buttoned-up stiff."

"Your secret's safe with me, Suit."

"That's my girl." He kissed her once more, then glanced at the laptop screen. "Let me just finish this up. I didn't think you'd sleep so late; I actually got more work done than

I thought I would. Five more minutes and I'll abandon work for the rest of the day. I'm all yours."

"Sounds great to me." She stretched her arms over her head, noticing how his gaze turned hungry as it went to her naked torso. "Do what you need to. I'm going to get some coffee." She kissed him once more and ran her hand over his chest, unable to keep from touching him before she got out of bed. The lack of warmth as the air hit her skin made her shiver. "Oooh crap, it's cold."

"It's supposed to snow later," he said, not looking up as he typed. "Starting around dinner time, I think."

"Awesome. But for now..." She went to his drawers, searching.

"What are you looking for, hon?" he asked.

"Pajamas. You must own at least one pair, though I've never seen you in them."

"That's because you always rip my clothes off and keep me naked. I'm just your sex slave. PJs have been unnecessary."

"A fair point. But do you have any?"

"Bottom drawer, babe."

Anna found a pair of flannel pajamas, a navy and royal blue plaid. She pulled on the top, which covered her almost to mid-thigh, and left the bottoms on the bed. "If you want them. I'm going to caffeinate now." Eyeing his slippers, she slid her feet in them. Though they were too big, they were better than bare feet on his cold floor. She grabbed her phone as she shuffled down the short hallway to the kitchen.

Out the window, she could see the sky was gray and heavy with clouds. Yup, snow was on the way. Nine days to Christmas, and snow on the way? That delighted her. As she made herself a cup of fresh coffee, she texted her sister-in-law.

Anna: Hi Cass, it's me

Anna: I was wondering if I could ask u something. Asking u before Sean since it's ur family

Anna: If I invited my guy to come with me for Christmas, would that be okay with u?

Cassandra: Reeeeeeeeally?

Anna: LOL yes really

Cassandra: Things are at that level, are they?

Anna: yes

Cassandra: GIVE ME MORE, WOMAN. DETAILS!

Anna: hahahaha

Anna: David is lovely. u'll like him. He always texts with proper grammar, like u

Cassandra: Then he's in, all right. I like him already.

Anna: So do u think ur parents would be ok with it if I bring him?

Anna: Also, do u think Sean will be cool or will he go into Jackass Big Brother Mode

Cassandra: I can't speak for your brother, but I'm sure my parents and aunts would be fine with one more body at *the table. Invite him.*

Anna: *That's great. Thx*

Cassandra: *Only thing is, you were going to sleep on the couch. Don't think the couch is big enough for two.*

Anna: *No worries. We'll take an Uber back into the city or get a hotel or something*

Cassandra: *If you say so.*

Anna: *Thank u, Cass. And… maybe break Sean in on the idea so he'll go easy on me?*

Cassandra: *Will do. You're welcome.*

Anna: *ur the bestest xoxo*

Cassandra: *And you're not off the hook. I still want details!*

Anna: *Later. I promise. I'm still with him right now, we're spending the day together.*

Cassandra: *On a Monday?*

Anna: *He called in to work so he could stay home with me*

Cassandra: *Oh wow. Your investment banker who's a workhorse? He's INTO YOU, woman.*

Anna: *u know what? He is. And I'm really, really happy about it ☺*

Cassandra: *Good for you. You deserve to be happy. I have to meet him.*

Anna: *u will next week at Christmas*

Cassandra: *Oh. Right. Okay. But I still want to hear everything!!!*

Anna: *u will, promise. Love u*

Cassandra: *Love you more. Enjoy your day together. Make it special.*

BY THE TIME they left his apartment, it was close to one o'clock and they were both starving. Bundled up in hats and heavy coats against the biting winter chill, David found the Uber he'd called and they went uptown. "This is totally cheesy," he said as they got out of the car in front of Rockefeller Center, "but it seemed like something you might enjoy, so…"

He took her hand and led her through the thick crowds to one of the restaurants directly next to the famous ice skating rink. With Christmas music playing overhead and twinkling lights all around, they had overpriced hamburgers and beers as they watched people outside skate. It was touristy and a cliché and Anna loved every minute of it.

During their meal, she invited him to spend Christmas with her, explaining how they'd be going to Cassandra's huge family gathering out on Long Island. He didn't hesitate as he accepted, reaching for her hand and squeezing it. Then he asked if he could bring her to his parents' house in New Jersey soon so they could meet her. She blushed and agreed.

As they exited the café, she asked, "What's next?"

"Skating at Rockefeller Center, of course." He steered her around, through the crowd.

"What? You can't be serious."

"I want to show you I'm willing to fall on my ass in front

of the whole world for you," he said. "Plus, it's so Christmasy. Quintessential New York Christmasy goodness. We'll have fun."

"But I haven't skated in years!" she cried.

"Me neither. Let's do it anyway."

They rented skates and carefully made their way onto the ice. Anna couldn't wipe the smile off her face. Christmas music played as they skated, or fumbled around, for forty-five minutes. She snapped pictures. They laughed, skated a bit, held hands, helped each other up when they fell down. She fell four times; he fell twice. He kept score. She made fun of him for keeping score. He promised to nurse her probable bruises when they got home.

When they'd returned their skates, he checked his watch. "I have a surprise for you, but we still have half an hour…" David glanced at his watch. "It's in Times Square. I know it's freezing out, but let's walk over."

"Sure." Anna slid her arm through his and kissed his cheek. "A surprise?"

"I'm not telling you, so don't bother trying to get it out of me. C'mon."

They walked through Rockefeller Center, past all the flags and lights and lit-up angels, until they came out on the Fifth Avenue side. It was a Monday afternoon but the sidewalks were packed with people, likely tourists and people who were playing hooky, like they were, to revel in the Christmas spirit. Holding hands, Anna and David strolled by

Saks Fifth Avenue to look at the famously decorated holiday windows.

"You're a good sport," she said.

"Why? What'd I do?"

"Indulging me with all the Christmasy things I enjoy. It's not your thing."

He shrugged it off. "Anna, just because I'm Jewish doesn't mean I don't enjoy Christmas. I very much enjoy the commercial aspects of it. Who wouldn't? It's lighthearted, colorful, fun. Magic is in the air. And let's face it, Christmas music is *much* better than Hanukkah music."

Anna had to laugh at that.

"I like Christmas fine," he said. "It just doesn't mean to me what it does to you, obviously. As I told you, my only beef with it is I don't like that it's swallowed up all of November and December, instead of just a few weeks of December, but what can I do?"

"Well, I just wanted you to know that I appreciate your taking me out and doing all these things and…" She stopped in her tracks as realization hit her. "As you've been trying to be a part of my world somehow."

"And you've done things to try to be part of mine. The mega menorah? Getting me a dreidel and gelt?" He looked down into her eyes. "We get the best of both worlds at holiday time."

"Lucky us," she breathed, captivated by him.

"Anna… we can be totally true to ourselves and be part

of each other's worlds too. There's lots of room there."

"You're right." She moved in to hug him tightly, pressing her face into the crook of his neck. "We can do that. I *want* to do that, David."

"Then we will." He slid his arms around her and held her close. "That's the best thing I've heard yet today."

They held each other for a minute before a thought hit her and she had to ask. "Are your parents going to care that I'm not Jewish? Your family?"

"No. Especially my mom. They just want me to be happy." He pulled back to meet her eyes. "What about you? Is your family going to care that I'm not Catholic?"

"They won't give one solitary fig," she said, and kissed him hard.

They took their time walking along Fifth Avenue, ducking into a Starbucks to grab cappuccinos to go. "So what is this surprise?" she asked.

"I'm stunned it took you this long to ask again," he said, laughing. "Wow!"

"So tell me!" she said, nudging him with her elbow. "Tell meeeeee."

"Nope. You'll see soon enough."

When they went back out into the late afternoon air, the bite of the chill went right through them. Anna shivered and said, "It got colder. And it smells like snow."

"You can smell the snow?" he asked, pulling his wool cap back onto his head.

"Yes. The air gets this... chill that goes into your bones, but it gets still, too. And you can smell the snow." She shifted her paper cup to her other hand so she could hold David's hand. "If you don't know what I mean, it's hard to describe it."

"I do know what you mean," he said. "But you smell it here, in the middle of the city? All I smell are fumes from cars and the occasional pretzel vendor. Your nose is more talented than mine."

They went up West 44th Street to get across to Sixth Avenue, emerging onto Times Square. The area was just as packed with people as Rockefeller Center had been.

"Doesn't anyone have work today?" David asked in consternation.

"It's a week to Christmas. They're all playing hooky like we are," Anna said with a smile. "So! We're here, we're in Times Square. What's the surprise?"

"C'mon, you." He tugged her by the hand and they walked some more, with the flashing billboards and lights and sounds and chaos of Times Square all around them.

"I know it's freezing out, and I'm sorry, but we have to wait a minute..." David pulled her toward the metal risers smack in the middle of Times Square, where people could sit and wait for theater tickets or just people-watch. They went halfway up and sat in the center of a center row, huddling close together.

"Drink your cappuccino," he said. "It'll help keep you

warm."

"Okay." She took a sip of her drink.

"Okay? That's it?" He looked at her quizzically. "That was too easy. Now I'm suspicious."

She laughed and snuggled close into his side. "Whatever this surprise is, I'm willing to wait. I'm here with you. This whole day has been the most romantic day I've had in... well, a very long time. Possibly ever. I'm happy. So, we wait."

He smiled and kissed her, his mouth warm and tasting of sugar.

"Look!" she said with delight. "Look up!" Snowflakes started to blow on the wind, the flurries light. "Do you see them?"

"I do. It's nice." He slid his arm around her shoulders and they rested against each other cheek to cheek. They watched the snow lightly fall as people talked and sang and yelled and moved around them, lights flashing and car horns honking, a whirl of color and sound and something magical.

"Okay!" David cried, shooting to his feet. "Baby, look." He grabbed her hand and pulled her up to stand. "This is for you, sweetheart."

He pointed to the left... and up. Anna didn't know what she was looking for at first, until it hit her, literally, like a neon sign. Because it was. Up on one of the buildings, one of the billboards read in big lit-up letters:

DAVID BEREN

LOVES

ANNA McKINNON

Anna gasped and her hands flew to cover her mouth. She stared at the billboard in shock and wonder. There were their names, in bold red letters, with hearts and snowflakes dancing all around the words.

David was such a private person. This… was a very, *very* public declaration of his love for her.

She gaped at him, stammering. "What—how—when did you do this?? Why did you do this?"

He cradled her face in his gloved hands as he gazed into her eyes. "Because I hate that you ever thought I'd be embarrassed for anyone to know I'm with you. Because I'm in love with you and wanted to shout it from the rooftops, tell the world. So… this was a way of doing that. I called in a favor. Friend of a friend." He peered harder. "I'm showing you I love you, in front of everyone. Hope you don't hate it…?"

Her eyes filled and she hiccupped out a watery laugh. "Are you joking?" She flung herself at him, hugging him as tightly as she could with their puffy jackets in the way. "This is just… I'm floored! What a romantic surprise! Thank you, baby. Thank you." She pulled back to kiss him over and over. "And, David… I love you too."

"Yeah?" His eyes rounded as a wide smile lit up his whole face. He held her close, arms locked around her waist. "It worked, then. Fantastic."

She laughed and kissed him. "I loved you already. I was just afraid to admit it." She smiled at him, touched his face. Her heart felt like it was bursting with light, like it couldn't hold all the love she felt.

"Merry Christmas, sweetheart," he whispered.

"Happy Hanukkah, Suit," she whispered back.

"It's the sixth night, so you're on point, it's still Hanukkah." He tweaked her nose playfully. "I love you, Anna. We're going to make this work."

"I know we are," she said. "And it's going to be the best walk on the wild side you've ever taken."

"I'll go anywhere, as long as I'm with you." He kissed her again and whispered against her lips, "*Bashert.* Meeting you… *bashert.*"

"I love that word," she said with a smile. "And I love you."

The snowflakes fell on them, covering them gently as they stood and kissed in the middle of the city for everyone to see.

The End

If you enjoyed this book, please leave a review at your favorite online retailer! Even if it's just a sentence or two it makes all the difference.

Thanks for reading *Holidays in Manhattan*
by Jennifer Gracen!

Discover your next romance at TulePublishing.com.

TULE
PUBLISHING

If you enjoyed *Holidays in Manhattan,*
you'll love the other books in....

The McKinnon Brothers series

Book 1: *All I Want for Christmas*

Book 2: *The Doctor's Love*

Book 3: *Marrying His Best Friend*

Book 4: *Love in Dublin*

Book 5: *Holidays in Manhattan*

Available now at your favorite online retailer!

If you enjoyed *Holidays in Manhattan*,
you'll love these other Tule Christmas books!

Royally Abandoned
by Sarah Fischer & Kelsey McKnight

Claiming the Cowboy for Christmas
by Kadie Scott

Christmas Flowers
by Sasha Summers

Available now at your favorite online retailer!

About the Author

Jennifer Gracen hails from Long Island, New York, where she lives with her two sons. After spending her youth writing in private and singing in public, she now only sings in her car and is immersed in her passion for writing. She loves to write contemporary romance for readers who look for authentic characters and satisfying endings. When she isn't with her kids, doing freelance proofreading, or chatting on Twitter and Facebook, Jennifer writes. She's already hard at work on her next book. Jennifer is a member of the Romance Writers of America and is active in the Long Island Romance Writers, as well as being a member of CTRWA.

Thank you for reading

Holidays in Manhattan

If you enjoyed this book, you can find more from all our great authors at TulePublishing.com, or from your favorite online retailer.

TULE
PUBLISHING

Made in the USA
Coppell, TX
27 September 2020

38825646R00146